THREE HOUSES IN ROME

THREE HOUSES IN ROME

Órfhlaith Foyle

Doire Press

First published in 2023

Doire Press
Aille, Inverin
Co. Galway
www.doirepress.com

Layout: Lisa Frank
Cover design: Tríona Walsh
Cover image: Julia Tochilina @ Shutterstock.com
Author photo: Taylor Doyle

Printed by Booksfactory
www.booksfactory.ie

ISBN 978-1-907682-95-7

We gratefully acknowledge the support and assistance of
The Arts Council of Ireland / An Chomhairle Ealaíon.

CONTENTS

To be alive and to be a 'writer' is enough.

— Katherine Mansfield, from her journals.

A BIT BOLD BUT NICE REALLY

Mass was over and Grandad came racing around the pub corner as we stood inside the shop door while his walking stick slid and scraped over the footpath.

Hello Grandad, we said when he appeared.

He told us we shouldn't be standing there. Go on upstairs to Granny. We filed past the Tayto crisp boxes and the shelves of sweet boxes. We hadn't stolen a damn thing but Grandad didn't trust us, so we ran up the stairs to the first landing and we could smell boiled eggs for tea. I went over to the landing's big window and looked out at the wet tarmac on the road. It was a Sunday night so there wasn't much to see but I liked looking at the wet road with the streetlights inside the puddles and I liked closing my eyes to hear things sound far away until a sick feeling came into my stomach and I was afraid.

My sister Ruby was jumping up the first step of the stairs to the second landing, then jumping back down. I put my tongue on the windowpane and breathed out, then the church bells rang out seven times for seven o'clock and Granny came out of the kitchen onto the first landing and said girls, your tea is ready.

I cut my egg into slices and Grandad said, would you look at her?

She doesn't like to mash it, Granny said.

Granny put on the kettle to make her and Grandad some tea and Ruby kicked out her legs underneath her table, munched her mashed egg and drank her milk.

Grandad said, what were you two girls doing in the shop?

Dad left us there, I said.

They're in for the night, Granny said as she put Grandad's mug of tea in front of him.

Can he not manage you for one night without your mother?

No, Ruby said.

Grandad took out his false teeth and sloshed them in a glass of water beside him on the table. He hated the taste of food on them after eating. He saw me looking at him and smiled a bit but not too much. Grandad didn't like being too nice with us. We were too noisy and played too many games, running up and down the top landing stairs, sliding down the bannisters, and last week we got out of the back-room window and walked around the stone yard there which belonged to the pub next door. Mr Teague hated our guts because Ruby went to the toilet there once and left a big poo.

So, who did it then? he yelled at Grandad. No bloody pussy cat shits that big!

Grandad told him to go away out of himself and not be annoying him. He said my girls are good.

Sometimes Ruby and I would imagine ourselves as giant girls who could step and skip over the roofs. When we grow up, Ruby said, we can be our own giants.

Whenever we were left in Granny's and Grandad's, Mam rang us from Dublin or wherever and told us to be good girls. We always said we were even though we stole sweets from the shop and long cigars to smoke down by the river. Sometimes we stole enough to sell and buy new slides for our hair or perfume that we would have to hide up on top of the wardrobe in our room and pretend that we had helped ourselves to one of our friends' mother's bottles instead. I loved the smell of summer rose perfume and Ruby loved the smell of dark autumn perfumes.

Of course we were found out and Grandad hit us with the back of his hand, then Dad did but he told Granny and Grandad, what could they expect from living above a sweet shop? He paid up for everything we had stolen, and we lost our pocket money all the way up to Christmas.

Ruby said, When we're older, we'll have our own sweetshop.

I don't want to have a sweetshop, I said.

Then we'll have something else, Ruby decided.

I emptied our bottles of perfume into the Shannon one day and Ruby beat me up in our bedroom. Granny was getting ready for the shop and she came running in to haul Ruby off me.

What? What? she yelled at us.

Nothing, we said.

Granny made us stay up in the bedroom all day. It used

to be Mam's bedroom when she was a girl like us but we never found anything that used to belong to her.

Oh, they would have got rid of my old things years ago, Mam said.

Granny said she was getting too old to be a babysitter and if your mother and father don't cop themselves on soon enough, they won't be able to run off without taking the two of you with them.

I told Ruby we had to be discreet.

Ruby said, I hate it when you use new words.

Ruby had a boyfriend that she used to kiss down at the river promenade. I sometimes went with them and waved at the tourist boats going up and down the Shannon, then I'd get bored so I'd head into the library and wait until Ruby had her face kissed off her and was bored too.

Both of us liked books but Ruby liked to be told the story of a book even more than she liked to read, whereas I just loved to read anything and everything. I'd read the back of a Rice Krispies box or marmalade jar at breakfast. I'd read Granny's shop order magazines and Mam's French detective books. I'd read Dad's farming magazines and news-papers. I'd read comics in shops until I was told to get the hell out. I'd read something on the toilet or while I was brushing my teeth. I'd read in school without the teachers knowing. I read the backs of newspapers where they print-ed pictures of dead people and all who loved them wrote them little poems. I imagined I was dead and Ruby wrote me a poem that made her famous, or Mam and Dad died in a horrendous car crash and I wrote a poem that when I died, it was hailed as the greatest poem ever about love and sadness.

I read Shakespeare, all of Charles Dickens, the Brontës,

who were Irish not English. I read *Little Women* but couldn't stand *Little Wives* or *Little Men*. I read *Anne of Green Gables* and thought hmmm, we live out in the countryside overlooking Lough Ree in Ballykeeran and it is even more beautiful than Green Gables, but I don't think we are happy there.

Mam said it was necessary for her to get away sometimes and Dad said off with you so. Then he'd bring us into Granny and Grandad would say well they better behave themselves, not like last time.

One of the last times I held onto my wee so tight in Phelan's newsagents/grocery shop around the corner. Ruby was taking too long to choose her *Just Seventeen* comic, then all of a sudden my wee whooshed out. It splashed everywhere and Mrs Phelan said oh my Jesus, my organic potatoes and sweet red peppers! Ruby laughed and laughed and said serves you right you big old pig. We ran down to the promenade and sat in the sunny part with my skirt up until my knickers dried off.

You weren't nice to Mrs Phelan, I said.

Hmmmpf, said Ruby and turned the next page of her *Just Seventeen* comic.

Mrs Phelan said if she had girls like us, she'd ship us off somewhere.

Granny said, the poor girl was short taken. If she had kept it in for longer, she could have ruined her kidneys. Grandad laughed, sure didn't she get extra fertiliser on her posh potatoes?

And even though Mrs Phelan said Ruby had stolen a magazine, there was absolutely no evidence because, after we had both read it, we tore it up and stuffed it into the rubbish bin outside the library.

Granny and Grandad were convinced that if Mam and Dad were more stable parents, then we'd be better girls. But Mam told Granny that marriage isn't like it used to be and Jesus, you had to have some bit of happiness in this life. Granny began to feel sorry for us and said we could start helping in the shop if we promised never to steal again. Ruby said it was worth it and if we did ever steal again, it would just be for ourselves.

Ruby and I were very good shopkeepers. We swept and dusted and arranged sweets and fruit and in summertime we sold ice creams. Everyone who came in loved our shop because it looked like it belonged in the century before last.

That's the nineteenth, I told Ruby.

I know that, said Ruby and pinched me.

One day Grandad lost his expensive red torch which helped him look under cars in his garage and he couldn't fix anything without it. It was missing for almost a week now and he was behind schedule. He roared at Granny who shrugged her shoulders and said Well, where did you last see it?

After tea, Mam rang us and said she hoped we weren't being bold. We said of course not and we were so good that Granny would be giving us ice cream wafers afterwards. Grandad was furious that whole evening and sat in front of the TV news trying to think back to where he left his torch. He asked if we had seen it. No, we said. He rang our Dad to see if he had borrowed it without telling him. Would you go away and shite, Dad shouted back.

It's bloody priceless that torch, Grandad told Granny.

Well, it isn't really, she told him.

She told us to have our showers and afterwards we sat at

the large window on the first landing and looked out while we licked our ice cream. I put my milky tongue on the windowpane while people were coming out of the post office.

You're eating them, Ruby said,

I'm kissing them, I said. I kissed a man with a cap and an old woman with a dog. I closed my eyes and felt that sick feeling in my stomach.

Everything went far away then. I imagined my legs growing so long, I could step over the promenade, jump over the Shannon, then stretch out my arms up into the sky and fly away and I wanted to cry for no reason at all.

Our room was cold when we went to bed, so we rubbed our feet up and down under our covers until our toes were almost warm. Ruby took a *Just Seventeen* from under her pillow and I lifted up Grandad's torch from under my bed, switched it on and it lit us up against the back wall. We waved at our giant heads.

I'm bored, Ruby yawned after a while. Tell me what you're reading

I told her a bit about the second half of the story of *Wuthering Heights*, about Hareton and Cathy because neither of us really liked the first Cathy or Heathcliff, but we thought the second Cathy was like us, a bit bold but nice really

I'm tired.

Me too.

I slept until I knew there was somebody in our room. He leaned over me, and I felt him pick up the torch from beside my pillow.

You little lovely bitches, Grandad said in wonderment.

He breathed hard and sat on my bed.

You little lovely bitches. I could feel him look at my face as he was saying it. He tapped the torch against the side of my head, and I concentrated on breathing exactly right. My chest went up and down in pretend sleep. I wanted to be far away, years away. I wanted to get up and climb outside this upstairs window and not fall down dead to the ground but just step over the post office on the opposite side of the street and then step over anywhere and I kept on exactly breathing, tap... tap... tap you little lovely bitch until it just stopped.

WELL, THEN

S adbh lay in bed and the ceiling, thick and white, lay above her. She was thirsty and drank some water from the glass on her bedside table, then patted her fingers on the edges of her duvet. It was early and the birds were singing in the trees outside her window. It was early and all she could think of was the attic. It lay above the ceiling, a room of rubbish and some treasure. Her mother's curtain collection of velvet wine-red, blood-orange, moss-green and dark-night-blue. There were chairs from various houses up there, and forgotten Christmas presents, as well as charity shop deals, books, fashion magazines, shoe collections, school reports and old copy books, decades-old information written on bank letters and bills.

She wanted to hurl it all out into a huge skip that would swallow everything. She imagined a cleared attic, only her father's long and high workbench left under the sky window, and she would put in another window and lie there under the stars at night. Ursa Minor across to Cassiopeia. She would stare at the stars and feel her body lift and spin as it used to do in her childhood. Lift and spin. She shut her eyes, but her body remained under the duvet and now the daylight had seeped through the curtains and onto her bed.

A toilet flushed then seconds later there was a knock.

'Yes, I'm awake, Mam.'

Her mother pushed open the door. 'Good morning pet. Did you sleep well?

'Hmm huh,' Sadbh said.

Her mother shut the door.

On the other side of the ceiling were four bucket chairs from the middle of the twentieth century, covered in faux, Middle-Ages tapestry cloth. If her mother ever died, Sadbh had decided she would keep those chairs.

She stood at the bathroom sink and avoided any direct looks at her face.

Her childhood rocking horse was up there. She'd keep that. He hadn't any saddle and his hair was matted grey instead of a straight silver colour and the last time she was up there, she had stroked his black velvet hide and noticed that his white wooden teeth were broken.

Perhaps some of the curtains too. The long wine-red velvet ones would be perfect to hang behind the front door at Christmas time. She could use the other coloured ones at other times or sell them on Done Deal.

She bent over the basin and splashed water onto her face and, for a quick second, she glanced at her reflection. She looked alright. She brushed her hair with her left hand since her other wrist was hurting.

'You're not wearing those?' her mother asked at the kitchen table.

'Hmmm huh.'

'They're not respectable or warm enough.'

'They're just leggings and the top is fine.'

'They are your yoga pants.'

'Mam, we are only going to Knock.'

Her mother spread some Pro Active on a slice of soda bread.

'And you're still doing your father's toes.'

'Mam, he can't bend down to do them himself. He has a huge stomach.'

'You make excuses for him all the time.'

'Mam...'

'You are breathing in all his stinking fungus. Your lungs will be destroyed.'

'I wear a mask.'

'I don't believe you. You lie to me. Every Wednesday, *I'm just heading down to see the girls* and, on the way back, you do his toes.'

'All I do is file them down and paint on the anti-fungal liquid.'

'And I know you'll be happy when I'm dead.'

'Mam, don't be stupid. As if I would.'

'You and your sisters are at me to clear out the attic, but I will do that in my own sweet time. It's my house.'

'I know. We all know.'

'I spent years having things taken off me, so don't think I'm going to let it happen now.'

Her mother spread some more Pro-Active on her slice of soda bread, then a sparser spread of whiskey marmalade.

Sadbh tossed a tea bag into her cup. The kettle had boiled before her mother said another word.

'You should wear your black pants and a nicer top than that one.'

'Okay. I will.'

'And your winter coat.'

'Right.'

'Ever since our marriage he's been taking things on me. He took my money on our honeymoon. I had to beg just to buy an orange in Rome.'

'We don't have to go to Knock, Mam.'

'And I don't trust your father's driving.'

The doorbell rang at half ten and her father stood in the doorway.

'Are you not ready yet?'

'Mam's putting on her coat.'

'You look well, Sadbh. Is it your hair?'

'I got it cut two days ago.'

Her father blew into his hands and stamped on the doorstep.

'I can drive us to Knock, Dad.'

'Why, do you think I'm senile?'

'No, it's just that sometimes you drive too close to the middle line.'

'Ah, I'll watch that.'

Her mother's bedroom door sounded shut and her mother stood at the top of the stairs.

'Sadbh, is my bag down there?'

'On the hall table, Mam.'

Her father drove close to the middle line a few times and mostly on purpose. He thought it was a joke. Sadbh watched the road and the oncoming traffic. Any minute now and we will crash but her father drove on, then missed the turn-off. He sailed right by for some metres, before he dragged the steering wheel to the right, did a sloppy U-turn, drove back and took the turn.

'Anyone could have missed that,' Sadbh said into the silence.

'Yes,' her mother said. 'It's stuck in there behind hedges.'

Sadbh sat into the back seat. *Okay, if we die, we die or at least we will be horribly injured. Fine. I will deal with it.*

'Yes, but you won't, will you?' her sister Maggie had said last week. 'You always back out of a confrontation with her. It's your house too since you put money from your settlement into it, so you have a right to upgrade the attic!'

Her other sister Juliet agreed. 'I have my council house. Maggie has the one her ex left her with. We're fine and you're the one doing the separate minding of both of them, and really you deserve the house because you haven't anything else.'

It was said before any of them could pretend it wasn't.

'I mean you're a brilliant art counsellor for teenaged drug addicts and abuse victims,' Juliet said

'Absolutely the best,' Maggie said.

'But you're alone, Sadbh.'

Sadbh sat in the back of her father's car. The rain had started and Vladimir Putin was on the car radio's twelve o'clock news invading Ukraine and threatening severe consequences to the West. Sadbh did not want to listen to him, so she concentrated on the interior of her mother's attic.

She could pack all the curtains into the tea chests for now, while her mother was alive, and providing she said yes. Most of the clothes could go back to the charity shops. Maggie suggested smuggling out bagfuls into the boot of the car whenever Mam was asleep in bed or asleep in front of the television.

'She'll know,' Sadbh said. 'She always knows.'

Sadbh would use her father's old workbench as her own art table. She'd have books and green plants for oxygen. She'd hide the tea chests full of curtains behind a Chinese screen and she'd have a king-sized bed with a couple of those bucket chairs placed...

'Oh... oh, they're mine,' Maggie told her.

'Yeah, and Mam said the white globe paraffin lamp from the 1920's is mine once she's dead.' Juliet said. 'And two of the tea-chests are mine.'

'You can have them now,' Maggie offered.

Sadbh often went up into the attic and sat amongst the black bags of clothes, curtains and rolls of carpet and rugs. Her rocking horse lay on its side underneath her father's long work bench surrounded by bags of Christmas decorations and a false Christmas tree in its box. There were extra roof tiles there and pillars of books and cooking magazines. In winter, Sadbh often lay back on the black bags and contemplated the roof. She would give it a Swedish colour courtesy of the painter Karin Larsson. Plain white in the middle, then bronze lines radiating to each side and corner. In the summer the roof boiled Sadbh as she collected stray clothes for her mother to sort through and bag again for Vinnie de Paul's or the Simple Simon shop.

No, she would not use a Chinese screen. She'd erect a plain one, then paint a deep red 'Rose of Love' in homage to Karin Larsson in the top centre and paint horizontal lines of blue, yellow, red and black all along the bottom edge... and she'd imagine living with some man like Carl Larsson on the banks of a cool, grey-green lake in a red-painted house... and she'd be normal, and she'd be loving...

'Here's Knock,' her father said.

'Knock,' Maggie had laughed when she heard. 'That place is one hundred percent the most miserable hole in all of Ireland.'

It was miserable. The wind pulled Sadbh's coat and rushed at her face as she and her parents approached the glass-fronted prayer centre that housed the old church's gable where Mary, St Joseph and St John the Evangelist had appeared to ordinary people in 1879. Everyone who saw them there said they were real, but now white statues stood in for Mary and her saints. Sadbh knelt and said to them, *Help me love.*

A soft 'dong' penetrated the prayer centre.

'That's the angelus bell from the Basilica,' her mother said.

She watched her parents creak to a standing position, creak down to genuflect and creak back up again. She followed them out into the wind and the Basilica bell rang a few more times. Sadbh had been in there once when she was fourteen and minding her baby sister, Maggie. Maggie had cried and cried so Dad had ordered Sadbh to take the blasted child outside and they wandered about, while the Mass blared through mounted speakers. Two old women watched Maggie tumble and totter while Sadbh ran after her. The two old women accosted Sadbh and she gazed at their wrinkles, their white hair under old-fashioned hats while their necks reminded her of screws twisting into their old, smelling, tweed coat collars.

'Is that your baby?' they said to her.

'No, she's my sister.'

The old women looked at each other, sucked their teeth and shook their heads.

'You're not minding her,' they decided. 'Not at all.'

'We're late for Mass,' her father said. 'How about confession?'

Confession was held in a near-subterranean chapel at the far end of the complex. It was all golden-brown wood inside and silent. Confessional boxes had evolved into confessional rooms and lined the interior. What do we do now, Sadbh wondered then noticed a woman signalling them closer. There were three confessional rooms ready but just take your time to prepare, she said and handed them a brochure each. Sadbh and her mother sat down while Sadbh's father wandered around, taking in the architecture.

'Don't forget all of your sins,' her mother whispered. 'Especially when you lied about your wrist pain just to get more settlement money.'

'But you all told me to lie!'

'I know but find out if that was a big sin.'

'But the money went into the house, Mam, and oil for winter, the new French Doors and the house insurance, and your new triple-glazed bedroom window, and the new flooring in the hallway, the dining and sitting rooms... and none of it has gone into the attic.'

'Just prepare for your confession, Sadbh.'

'Mam, sometimes I think you love God far too much.'

Her mother went silent for seconds then said, 'I will not
be bullied into clearing out the attic. I had enough of that
with your father.'

'But Mam, all that stuff is just sitting on top of us.'

'It's my stuff. I will not have you bullying me.'

'I'm not Dad, Mam.'

'You love him more. After everything he was.'

'He's lonely and old, Mam.'

'He beat me until I was a bloody mess on my honeymoon.'

'I know.

'And he beat you because you were useless at maths.'

'He beat us all, Mam and now he's sorry.'

'Hmm. Look at him, wandering around admiring God.'

'I'm going in,' Sadbh said.

The confessional room had three chairs. The priest sat
in one behind a wooden mesh screen, so Sadbh sat on the
chair in front of that. The third chair was meant for one-on-
one confession. The kids who came to her sat in chairs like
that. They stared at her wondering how she'd magic them
normal and instead she taught them to draw, paint or sculpt
their feelings. Sometimes they spat at her. One even said he'd
fuck her if he was drunk enough. She failed with him. He was
taken away and given to someone else.

She often wanted to tell them they weren't the first to
be beaten, abused, derided, made little of and they weren't
the first to taste their own blood in their mouths, or go to
school with their hair roots and scalp throbbing in pain, trying to be normal and watching the teacher smile while you
are thinking in your mind *you don't know what I'm really like
and you don't know what my Dad is like.*

Dumbo. Stupid. A head like a sieve for maths. Christ, you can't even think, can you?

The one who said he wanted to fuck her. She imagined him about twenty years older and that had kept her heart warm for a while, until a man met her in a pub one night and he stuck his hand inside her bra, and she allowed it there for perhaps ten seconds wanting to know what to feel but he was too big, too hard and she vomited into his mouth.

'Bless me Father for I have sinned,' she began.

'I can't love anyone. I've tried but it's mainly going through the motions. I mean love for a man, I suppose. I just go cold and want to be eleven years old again and no one can touch me.'

'I can love my family. We all can manage to love each other but sometimes I lose the knack of it and I am amazed anyone can love anyone at all.'

'I have this thick rotten thing covering my heart and I often imagine my mother dead, so I tell myself to really love her now, even when she will not shut up talking about the past and all her hate for my father and for the useless men in my sisters' lives and how she has always expected me to be good and I have let it become a disease inside of me... this thing covering my heart... it drips down into my stomach and my fists.

Sadbh took a breath. 'She won't let me do up the attic for my art. I got some money a while ago and did a good bit with the house, but she says the attic is hers and it is full of all the things she bought to make herself better. She has curtains there because she loves colour and furniture, and old beautiful lampshades. I just want somewhere to breathe but it is all useless really. Rugs she'll never use, a whole roll of carpet she wants to put down in the spare room and hasn't, even though it's been in the attic for five years. Bags and bags of clothes she kept buying in charity shops.

'I just have to wait until she's dead.'

Sadbh concentrated on the wooden mesh screen. 'I haven't been to confession for years and she's guilting me into going to Mass because no one else will drive her there. She says I'll ask for forgiveness and love God on my deathbed. But if I can't really love anyone, how can I love God?'

Sadbh stopped talking and stared through the wooden mesh.

The priest opened his mouth with a pop of spit and breath. He cleared his throat.

'Have you ever been violent with your mother?'

'No, of course not. Just myself. I punch myself.'

'Where?

'In my head, my face now and again.'

You'll tell me to love myself now, she thought.

'Do you want to love?'

'Yes.'

'Well, then.'

'Then what, Father?'

'You are already loving,' he answered.

He gave her an Our Father and an instruction to medi-ate on the glorious heart of Mary, mother of Jesus.

Oh God, Sadbh thought and left the confessional.

Her parents were nowhere to be seen.

She walked over to where a sculptor's wooden replica of a Skellig monk's beehive stone hut stood on a red-carpeted corner. It was called a meditation cell. Step inside its sliding door, shut it and sit for fifteen minutes and contemplate your place with God. A note on the door declared that it was shut until further notice.

Sadbh wandered towards the pews facing the altar.

Well, then, the priest's words stuck in her mind.

Well, then.

She knelt for a while in front of the altar, then sat back and looked up at the roof that soared to a point. Perhaps it's meant to make your soul soar, she thought. She tried it there with her heart, willing it to soar against her breastbone, breaking it through the roof's point, soaring to the sky through the miserable clouds and into infinity with Ursa Minor and Cassiopeia and all the stars for ever and ever Amen.

LOVE IN MOSCOW

In the Arbat, in a Russian teahouse, while the others were talking about Lenin, Norah Lally was busy glancing through her Kremlin brochure, half-conscious of the whispered conversation on dollars for roubles, half-glimpsing at her father as he chewed on thick blinis, then poured his hot tea from the mini-samovar that was clamped to the café table.

'Won't we be late?' she reminded him.

He nodded *who cares*, then coughed as a blini stuffed his throat. Norah wondered if she should make a show of trying to save him before he swerved in his seat and coughed up a mess of blini onto the floor.

Joss and Neal, two brothers from Ontario, and Lucy and Cath, two teacher best friends from Dunedin in New Zealand remained still and did not drink, eat or move until they saw that Norah's father was going to make it.

'No real hurry,' Neal said. 'That dead coot is a mummy.'

'I don't want to spend my whole afternoon queuing to see him,' Cath said.

'If it's even worth it,' Lucy said.

'They pump chemicals into him every year to keep him,' Norah said.

'It's just his skin and some glass eyes,' her father said. 'But that's history.'

Joss grunted a laugh

'I'd prefer go see a poet's house,' Cath said.

'You and your poets,' Neal said as if they had been sleeping together for years instead of just two nights.

'Norah likes her poets.'

'Yeah, which ones?' Joss asked.

Norah grabbed names from her head. 'Pushkin. Tsvetayeva, Akhmatova.'

'I don't do poetry,' Joss said. 'You look like a poet though.'

'Thanks,' Norah said.

Lucy stood up and grabbed her coat and hat. 'Are we seeing Lenin or what?'

Norah's father was the last to exit the teahouse. 'I left a tip,' he told the others.

They all shrugged, then shifted their eyes to view different sections of the Kremlin vista.

'Something about those red bricks,' Lucy said. Then she looked at Norah. 'Your Dad said you're a history nut.'

Norah shrugged. 'Yes.'

'Her mother and I are really proud of her,' Norah's father said.

'Teachers too, huh?' Lucy guessed.

'Maths. Geography,' Norah heard her father reply before she walked on ahead of them all, taking off her glasses, squinting one eye then the other and saw how useless her right eye was when it focused on the Kremlin wall. Her father's voice carried on the freezing air, and she kept walking towards Lenin's tomb, carefully planting one booted foot before the other, mindful of the ice that cracked and sped lines in front of her. Her father's voice was talking about love. It's a mission of love, she heard him say then heard Cath and Lucy coo back all interested. Even Neal's voice clambered in.

'Love. Yeah?'

'Yeah,' Cath told him. 'The do-or-die kind, buddy.'

Neal 'Slightly psychopathic if you ask me. Ow!'

Joss said, 'Less of the domestic violence, you two.'

He jogged up to Norah. 'I don't believe in love, do you?' but she was concentrating on a small man disguised as Vladimir Lenin who darted in and out of the line, calling 'Coming to visit me, dear ones?' He tip-toed, marched then goose-stepped cooing at the queueing tourists' phone cameras, real cameras, even their woolly hats with thick ear flaps.

'It all went to shit after me, dear ones.'

'Crazy bastard,' Joss remarked.

Lenin spun on his toes. 'I made Russia! And that bully boy tyke Stalin destroyed it!'

Two Russian guards walked out of the ziggurat tomb, lit cigarettes and smirked as the tourists babbled. Norah unwrapped a bit of chocolate from her pocket and let it melt at its own pace on her tongue.

'My dear girl,' Lenin cried out to her, arms ready to pluck her into his dance and she smelled coffee on his breath. His fingers barely touched her wrist when he was plucked instead, head-jammed down onto the ground, his arms hiked upwards, one solder's foot on the nape of Lenin's neck.

Joss slotted his hand into the small of Norah's backbone, just under her coat belt.

'Come on.'

Norah moved up the queue.

The entrance was dark inside and a soldier said something to her.

'What?'

His gun butted her hands out of her pockets, he snapped her glasses from her face, studied her ears, her glasses again, peering at the different thickness of the lenses before giving them to his comrade who examined them also, decided *Nyet*, and, handing them back to her, jerked his head towards a descending stair.

She obeyed but halted halfway down until her father and the others appeared.

'Poor pretend-Lenin,' Norah said.

'He'll be alright,' her father said.

'Hey,' Joss said, moving up close to her. 'Been meaning to ask what kind of name Lally is because it sounds like it's all tongue to me.'

His grin fissured his face from his lips to his eyes.

'Lallypop, lallypop,' he sang.

'Idiot,' she said and turned away from him. The line ahead of her had parted into two circles. The outer one was made of tall people and the inner one, which she was now herded into, held all the short people.

'Ah... so I can look over your little head,' Joss whispered.

She ignored him and gazed towards Lenin lying in his glass coffin under a stepped stone slab. He has red hair, she noted. Her Kremlin brochure hadn't mentioned that. His face was stretched pale, the way plasticine stretched. He was completely dead looking.

'No photos!'

'Ah give over,' said a woman in front of Norah and fast-clicked her camera phone, daring the young soldier who then raised his gun and knocked the woman's phone out of her hand.

'That's an iPhone 11,' she shrieked.

Everyone stopped walking.

'He's going to step on it,' Joss said over Norah's head.

The soldier dragged the phone closer with his right foot, picked it up, undid its safety cover, dropped it to the floor, smiled at the woman then aimed the butt of his gun.

'Milking it,' Joss admired.

The gun butt smashed down, down again and down once more until the iPhone spun sideways, bits of glass flying.

'You... you... you... Putin' and the man she was with put his hand over her mouth.

Everyone's breath puffed out while the soldier stood and waited until the man pushed his wife onwards. The soldier shouted and everyone moved forward.

Norah glanced around for her father. He was behind Joss. He smiled, raising his eyebrows. Stupid woman.

Norah turned back to Lenin and craned on tiptoe. His black suit looked new under the tomb's lights. She decided that his mouth must be invisibly cemented tight and straight, and she knew false eyeballs were in place to prevent his eye sockets collapsing. Hmm, she thought then followed her line out into the Red Square.

She stood in the cold wind, waiting and Joss came out first, smiling while Norah's father hung back with the New Zealand teachers, all three exchanging numbers on their mobiles.

'What does he mean "a mission of love"?'

'My mother ran away, and he wants her back,' Norah answered.

'Why did she run away?'

'She got fed up I suppose.'

'Of what?'

'Just of being married. At least that's what she said on the phone a while ago.'

'I don't believe in marriage,' Joss said.

She looked at him. 'I don't care,' she said.

She sounded bold as brass and liked it.

He smiled. 'I'm just putting it out there.'

'Okay.'

'Hey, how old are you?'

'Twenty-one.'

'You look younger.'

'It doesn't matter, does it?'

'No, not at all.'

Lucy and Cath approached with Norah's father and Neal following.

Joss said, 'Hey, how about St Basil's?'

'Saw it yesterday,' Norah's father said.

'Okay,' Joss said to Norah. 'So, I'll buy you a beer at this thing tonight?'

'I don't drink beer,' she said and licked her lips against the cold.

He leaned forwards and kissed the corner of her mouth and sipped up some of her saliva.

'Let's go,' he told the others then lead the way across Red Square.

The hotel foyer was full of a new load of tourists as well as a new batch of prostitutes, blonde- and black-haired women, some in small, tight dresses, others in longer ones. Most wore short or full-size fur coats and high-heel sandals with red-painted toes on show. Norah watched them introduce themselves as translators and city-guides to the tourists. They had studied English in Europe, in Hungary, in Slovakia, in London. *Yes. London is so beautiful. You are London, yes?*

'No,' Norah's father had told them a few nights ago. 'Ireland... actually... Sydney. In Australia.'

'Ah,' they nodded and translated each to each while Nora watched them.

'And this?' they said about Norah, studying her fake, grey fur ankle-length coat, her red face because of the cold outside and stuffed-up heat inside. She was sweating a little under her eyes and on her top lip. *No lipstick*, their eyes said. *That thing about her neck. Wool? How fat her face is. How young. How nothing.*

'My daughter,' Norah's father answered.

Their lips curled up. *Her glasses — too big for her eyes!*

'They think you're my girlfriend,' her father laughed. 'They'd be silly enough to think I'd pick you.'

It was said as a joke.

Their room smelled of strawberries and every surface had been polished. Norah took off her coat, then hunted out a book from her suitcase to read. It wasn't anything much. Just some Moscow information book she had bought the day before they flew out of Sydney. She sat on her bed and flicked through the pages.

'Old Lenin was a bit of an anti-climax,' her father said.

He threw himself on his bed and scrolled through his phone. 'Nothing,' he said.

Norah nodded to herself. 'She might be busy doing stuff,' she said.

'Maybe.'

Norah turned a page loudly. 'She might not want to see us. Maybe she'll laugh at us for coming after her and I'm twenty-one, Dad. It's not like I'm thirteen all over again. I just came with you as if I was a little girl.'

'So?'

She turned from her page to see her father's face lying sideways, looking at her.

'Maybe I should have stayed with Rory and Ciara.'

'You said you wanted to see your grandparents.'

'I know but I just feel...' She stopped talking because she knew he wasn't interested in what she felt, and she didn't know how to say what she felt. She tried to think her way through the feeling but all she saw inside her head was a mass of grey, spongy pulp.

I'm living on my nerves, Norah's mother's voice screamed through the grey pulp.

Do I even fucking care, Nora's father screamed back.

Norah put her head against the hotel wall.

Why did I come? The grey pulp in her head moved like slow fat and she thought how stupid she was to have come. She was the eldest, but she still wanted to believe that her parents were worth something together. Rory said you got all that crap from books. Ciara said she wanted to study for school exams which everyone knew was a lie. She had plans to be on Bondi beach with her mates.

'Don't forget I really love you, Norah,' her mother had told her, looking upwards because Norah was standing on her study table, reaching for a book from her bookshelves. She remembered how funny her mother had sounded because she said she was just heading out for a while.

'Alright Mum,' Norah said.

Her mother touched Norah's ankle, then tapped along her barefoot to her toes.

'I really love you, Norah.'

She phoned some hours later from the airport. She loved Norah, Rory and Ciara. She loved them all but was going mad with him.

'He'll come and get you,' Norah warned.

Something just as grey and just as hard as the grey pulp in Norah's head now filled Norah's heart.

'Dad,' she said.

'Hmm?'

'I don't think it's a mission of love, Dad.'

He laughed and she remembered Joss's tongue licking the corner of her lips.

'That's exactly what it is, Norah.'

Norah stretched her legs under the bed's duvet, thrilling her toes with the cold sheet. She would kiss Joss tonight. She would imbibe vodka and kiss. She would pretend she mistook it for plain water to dilute the restaurant's berry cordial and note the glint on Joss's teeth. She presumed his neck would be warm and beneath his Adam's apple would be fuzzy and tickle her nose. She would kiss him outside the restaurant, out in the middle of a building site where the restaurant lay hidden from authorities and dealt in USA dollars. Her father would disappear and Norah, her head sozzled in vodka, would allow Joss to take her hand and lead her out into the cold deep dark, against an idle cement mixer and kiss and kiss and kiss.

IN LORIENT

I was in Lorient to meet up with my brother, Max. I had been there for two days wandering in and out of functional cafes and every so often I walked down to the beach to where kids hung out at the war bunkers, drinking, swearing, having sex. I sat down on the sand and watched the sea come in, then go out. I was waiting. I dug my toes into the wet sand and I waited for Max to answer my texts. The drunk kids got fed up of me sitting there and threw their beer cans so I lifted my right arm, cocked my thumb and aimed my index and middle fingers right at the drunken teens and I yelled, 'Hey Bitches! Better Respect. Pow! Pow!'

Then I got up and walked away. It was night and my head was pounding. Men looked at me as I passed them out on the footpaths. The French love correct behaviour. They adore manners but I ploughed on and through. I heard *merde, putain,* and

fuck you. I laughed at them and walked on to my hotel room.
It was a stuffy night. I shoved open the windows and stared at
the sky. Lights were on all over the place, so the sky wasn't as
real as it should have been with just the stars on fire. I bit my
fingernails for a while. I had a shower and I wandered naked
in front of the open window. Then I put on a red dress. Then I
put on knickers. Then I leaned outwards on my balcony window. A few men looked up at me. I caught their looks, then I
looked away. I lit a cigarette and blew smoke into the air.

My phone pinged with a text.

I counted to ten then reached for my phone and opened
the text.

Hey how are you? This takes time. I talk to him, ciao Sabine.

I glanced over my window balcony and smoked for a
while longer. Then I texted:

I am here for another day. Tell him I love him.

I stared at the words as I counted the seconds. Then I
pressed send. Then I sat on the edge of my bed, switched on
the television and watched a Breton festival report, but all the
time my mind was on Max.

*You must understand. It is difficult for him but I tell him,
she is your sister.*

Yes, I replied. *Of course I am. I am the eldest of his three
sisters.*

I deleted the last sentence.

A dog barked so I glanced out my balcony window and
saw an old woman leading a tiny terrier. She stepped into a
late-night café and her dog followed. I watched them from my
balcony and through the café window I saw the old woman
sit on a chair, then seat her dog on her lap. They were served
tea, ham and cheese. It seemed so ordinary. I went back to the

television, stared at it for a few seconds then turned the sound up so I could fall asleep thinking everything was normal.

The next morning I ate a croissant dunked in hot chocolate, then I went out for some sea air. There was a cold wind and a man with one leg stopped to heave breadcrumbs into the air for the seagulls. He nodded at me and I nodded back. He watched me for a while as I walked up and down the beach, then he yelled something, but I didn't bother to understand him. After a while he gave up and hopped away on his crutches.

I stood for a while longer and stared at the grey rolling sea, then I texted,

If he does not come I can go to where he lives.

The reply was quick. *No please. I am talking to him. Be optimistic, ciao Sabine*

I was having a late-morning coffee in a Quick fast-food restaurant when the last text came through

Salut! 6 pm at The Galway Inn. Perhaps you have been there? They serve good food. The children love it when their father brings them there.

I had prepared myself to meet Max in any situation. I had playacted in front of the mirror in my bathroom. I had experimented with my tone of voice in supermarket queues. I walked into pubs, ordered a gin and tonic, sat somewhere near to the entrance so I could imagine seeing Max for the first time in twenty years.

Hello Max.

Hi.

I never got him to say my name in my imagination. It was stuck in his throat, my throat, rooted hard.

The Galway Inn wasn't busy, so I ordered a coffee and waited and watched each time the pub's door opened and closed.

Six minutes. We are parking. Ciao.

When he came through the door, I thought there he is. Tall, wearing a North Face jacket. His strawberry blond hair was paler. His freckles were numerous. He approached and said, 'Hi.'

I lifted my arms and put them around his back. He did the same. Then we let go and his two kids held out their hands to shake mine.

'This is Inez. This is Antoine.'

'Hello,' I said.

Then Sabine kissed both my cheeks. 'Finally, no more texts, yes?'

She steered me back to my chair and sat next to me.

'Oh, don't worry about Max. He is with the children. We have to talk a little first, yes?

'I have presents for the children,' I said and handed a red carrier bag across the table to Max. His eyes did not flick over mine once. A hole opened in my stomach like a sneer. What did you expect, you stupid bitch?

Inez and Antoine squealed and unwrapped their gifts. I had gone for the generic mainstays of a colourful wacky encyclopaedia of the Irish language, pampooties from the Aran Islands and Irish linen unisex shirts for both of them.

'Thank your aunt,' Max said.

The waiter came in the middle of their thanks, so they switched to calling out 'Frittes, frittes, Papa! Frittes!'

'Mum and Dad send their love,' I told Max.

'Yeah,' he said. 'That's nice. Tell them I love them back.'

'I am having a vegetable curry,' Sabine announced to the

waiter. She looked at me.

'The same,' I said.

'Frittes and beer for me,' Max said.

'You look well, Max,' I said.

He nodded but kept his eyes on his kids. 'Don't touch your presents with ketchup fingers! Hey. You know the drill. Hey.'

Sabine touched my arm. 'I am so happy to be able to speak to you in real life,' she whispered and I glanced at Max's profile, wondering if his ears were listening. 'And before you speak with him, I have to know what you are going to say to him.'

I looked at her.

'It has taken me so long to get him to this happy place where he is now. So nothing should be destroyed, should it?'

'Oh,' I said.

Sabine smiled. 'He suffered so much more than you or your sisters. I know you all suffered and your father's temper was immense but he suffered more, no? The beatings...'

'We were all beaten,' I said.

'Yes, but he was beaten more.'

'I was the first,' I said.

'Yes, but he was beaten the hardest,' Sabine said.

And I wanted to laugh in her face while my spine prickled up into a thousand serrated edges under my skin and I marvelled at how well Max had assembled his defences.

Let it go, my sisters had advised me. *Let him go. Let him die in years to come and none of us will go to his funeral.*

But I was the first, I reminded them. And I was supposed to have stopped him.

I ate little of my vegetable curry, studying my brother as

he spoke with his kids and a few times he directed a smile towards Sabine, who after her third smile at him, turned to me and said,

'He was so afraid to come tonight but I told him as I have told you, she is your sister and she loves you.'

I laughed.

Sabine smiled. 'Yes?'

Sabine had a middling-sized face with a pointed chin and large blue eyes. She had blonde hair cut into spiky layers that covered her ears and grazed her shoulders.

'Twenty years is such a long time to finally say hello,' she said.

'Well, I was growing up, then I had college and more college.'

'And you're the only sister to visit Max.'

'Air tickets are expensive since Covid.'

'What do you want to talk to him about?'

'Just things,' I said.

She smiled. 'I don't want him upset.'

'Oh,' I said.

'And anyway, it's a school night and we'll be leaving soon.'

As if she had rung a bell, Max stood up saying, 'Okay kids. Home time.'

'Max,' I said.

He looked at me. 'Sorry. The kids have school tomorrow.'

'I want to talk with you,' I said.

He was handing over his card to pay for the dinner and shrugged, then smiled.

'You look really good, you know.'

That hole in my stomach tightened to a crack as Inez and Antoine kissed my face au revoir, followed by their mother who squeezed and patted my shoulder goodbye. Max walked out of the pub and we all followed.

'You should visit the WW2 bunkers before you leave,' Sabine said.

I pushed past her to where Max stood holding Inez's hands as she danced on tiptoe.

'Max.'

Inez looked at me. 'You have the same skin as me.'

'What?' I said.

Inez nodded at my lower bare arm visible because of my loose cardigan cuff.

'Creamy white like me, see?

I felt the hole in my stomach tighten hard to a crack.

'Do you remember that sweatshirt with no sleeves you used to wear, Max? You had 'Urban Toreador' ironed on it from Dire Straits, remember?'

He was smiling down at Inez and shaking his head. 'No.' Then his eyes gazed past mine, so I made them come back.

'You thought you were something,' I said.

I stared at him, right into the seventeen-year-old boy he had been. When he had known what he had done. When I had known too. When every time I went to tell, the words stuck inside me because everything I was had now boiled dark and it kept boiling until I starved or gorged, or cut or hit and until now, when everything had nowhere to go and I wanted to tear my hands into his heart, unroot it and stamp it flat.

'I was a kid,' he said. 'All kids think they're something.'

'You're nothing,' I said. The crack inside me tightened further. 'You're nothing. You're not even a name to us any-more.' The crack inside me smoothed except for tiny fissures where I decided something good could grow there after all.

I let him go. I went down to the beach and stood ankle-deep in the fast surf and I let him go. *Let him be nothing*, I screamed out over the sea. *Let him be nothing but a name that will die someday!* I kept screaming until another scream answered.

'Hey Bitches! Better Respect. Pow! Pow!'

A girl waved at me from the crowd of partygoers at the WW2 bunker. *Come on, come on!* So, I walked up there and she handed me a can of beer and some kitchen paper to wipe my tears and my face, then she sat me down next to her and her friends.

They had a fire going and some guy decided to play guitar. I nearly laughed at the clichéd silliness of it all but I stopped myself, because I had to breathe and I had to keep on breathing because what else is there but nothing?

I had to live. I really had to live.

The guitar was beautiful. Everything was beautiful. The sea smell, my toes in the sand, the fire, the beer. I focussed on the bluest flames of the fire until I felt as light as air and I remembered I was wearing my red dress, so I danced and I kept on dancing.

JOSEPH NOW AND EVER AFTER

After I killed Barry Salmon, I made coffee then I cut some bread and cheese. I added tomatoes and handed the plate to Poppa.

'Where's the ham?'

'It's off. I gave it to the dog.'

No One lifted his head from the fire hearth. I rubbed it. I felt the bones of his skull, then I threw up coffee and marrowfat peas from the day's dinner.

Poppa did not look round from the TV.

'Going out for a while, Poppa.'

No One and I went into the village to the garage and grocery store. Barbara, the owner's wife, never minded the dog coming in as well.

'Hello,' she said to me. 'What have you been up to today?

'Nothing much.'

'Minding that father of yours?

'Hmm mmm. Is that today's soda bread?'

'This afternoon's batch, Joey.'

She smiled at No One, leaned her thin chest over her till counter and gave the dog a treat of chicken meat.

Her shop was never well-stocked. She and her husband Barry had plans to take over the closed-down pub about two kilometres down the road and turn it into a high-class deal. I went to school with Barry. We had both been good at football. I smiled at Barbara. I remembered kissing her before Barry ever did.

'So, how's life, Joey?'

'Joseph,' I said, 'I'm okay,' I said.

She smiled. I knew her smile off by heart. It said all sorts of things to me. If only I had taken you instead of Barry. If only you hadn't run off to a life in Dublin. If only you hadn't come back. If only you hadn't been in the car accident and if only something hadn't happened to the brain inside your head.

I wanted to push her hair back behind her ears like I used to do.

'Don't stare Jo-y-seph,' she said. 'It isn't nice.'

I stared up at her shop lights instead. They blinked and zig-zagged at me. No One whined and nudged his muzzle into my knee.

'See you now, Joey,' Barbara said.

No One and I walked out into the sun and back along the coast road. Tourists smiled over at us, thinking we were the flavour of the day. They asked directions to the castle ruins.

'The Spanish Armada called in here, didn't they?' a tourist asked me.

'I couldn't tell you,' I said.

'What's your dog's name?'

'No One.'

'What?'

'He just turned up one day and no one was with him. So that's what we called him.'

It was late summer and the green in the trees was turning deep and thick and lovely. I stood and stared at it for a while, and I tried to remember proper ways to describe what I was seeing. If I reached up and felt the green, it would turn soft between my fingers but there would also be small slivers of hard fibre inside, and I would have to press hard and harder to make them snap.

No One sighed.

'Okay,' I said. 'We'll go home.'

Poppa was in the garden digging up the ground. He looked older than this morning. He smiled so I smiled.

'I think there is a rat around somewhere. The dog might find it.'

'Hmmmm,' I said and went inside. I turned down the TV and went into the kitchen, turned on the radio to RTE One and listened to the news. It was the same as most days and so was the weather. I opened the fridge and took out some sausages for later. I peeled potatoes and put them in water.

Poppa came in. 'Did I bring in the runner beans?'

'There aren't any,' I said.

'I dug them up,' he said.

I looked at the wrinkles on his forehead.

'You ate them earlier,' I said.

'I did?'

'You cooked them in butter the way Momma used to cook them for you.'

He looked at me and maybe half-lied. 'Oh, I did, that's right.'

'It's the not knowing,' she said.

'I know,' I said.

'He's often not come back for a few days, but this is worse. Maybe he's left me for another woman.'

'I doubt it,' I said as I reached for the tomato sauce.

'He stopped touching me, Joseph.'

I stared at her as she examined her till.

'What made me say that... Jesus.'

'He'll come back,' I said.

'Maybe I won't have him back.'

'I'll take this, Barbara and some of those apples.'

She zinged up what I owed her.

I stared at the rims of her blue eyes and at her mascara full of eye lashes. I knew they would spike my lips if I kissed them, and she would spit. Not like the old days when she miaowed.

'Stop staring, Joey,' she said.

Two Guards called to our door with questions that I could answer fine.

'We loaned ourselves out to Barry whenever he needed us,' I agreed.

One of the Guards leaned forwards to look at my mother's photograph on the mantlepiece.

'She always told me what books to read from the library,' he said.

'Must be hard living without her,' the first Guard said, first to Poppa, then to me.

I knew how people talked about us. Sometimes Poppa forgot himself and wandered about looking for an open pub to meet his old friends even though the pub is boarded up and all his old friends have disappeared. Sometimes someone would bring him back to me. Other times I would go looking. The doctor told me it was a slow decline. You are at your level, now Joey. He must find his.

'Yeah, lovely woman,' the second Guard said after clearing his throat.

Me and Momma standing outside in the garden. I was ten. She was about thirty-nine. She had been a teacher. She said she married Poppa because there was a hole in her life and nothing else could cover it but him. She said that was love.

I said, 'Maybe you should go now, Guards. I don't want Poppa to get upset.'

They raised their eyebrows at each other then said,

'Don't you remember us, Joey? Matt and Christy?'

'No.'

'We were in school with you. We were there after you crashed your car... the one your Mum died in; you remember that now?'

I am driving the car. I am driving it fast. A new car from my big architect's job in Dublin, showing off now back in the west of Ireland in a place full of hills and sheep and spread-out townlands and nothing in between except sea and sand and wind and rain. See how fast it goes, Momma. Oh, Joseph the green is going by too fast, and the road, Joseph, oh mind the road. You hit a sheep, Joseph. You hit more and the now the car is turning, and I can see your scream as you open your mouth,

Joseph, and my head is snapping back and all my fingers stick out and my body is flying out through glass and so are you, and your head crunches onto the ground and you live, and I die.

We laid her out in the front room. She was pale and beautiful. Poppa hit me the day of her funeral, then he held my head and cried.

Poppa said, 'Your mother has made soda bread, if you'd like to give the Guards some.'

'They're going now,' I said.

Christy tapped Momma's photograph. 'Lovely woman.' He tapped her photograph so hard it fell face down. He picked it up, brushed it against his sleeve and put it back.

Matt said, 'Well we have to ask these questions since you two were probably the last to see Barry Salmon.'

Poppa lifted his grey damp eyes. 'When did we last work there, Joey?'

'Almost a month since, Poppa.'

'Must be hard to work on land that used to belong to you,' Matt said.

'It's fine,' I said.

I shut the door after they left, and Poppa went on the internet to look at women while me and No One decided to go for a walk. I bit off a piece of chocolate from my pocket. No One devoured a dead bird, claws up and almost fresh.

We walked down the green lane, past the Crowe's summer house, down towards the bay with its large rocks and its level blue sea. Barry's body lay behind one of the rocks. I finished my chocolate then No One and I jumped down onto the sand. Barry's body was where I had left it. It still looked like him except for its green and purple colour skin.

'Barry.'

Barry had laughed once because he knew I still loved Barbara.

'With that useless head of yours, would you even know what to do anymore?'

Barry laughed because Poppa, No One and me would come to his backyard on the days he had work for us and he'd stand in his kitchen door, munching rashers on toast, talking about the land that had once belonged to my mother. He'd watch Poppa walk on the land.

'Your old man never knew how to treasure things, did he Joey?' He looked at me.

He thought he had a brain better than me.

'You're different from the old Joey Carstairs, aren't you?' he said.

I shrugged.

'You were all swank and business when you came back for your *vacations*. Maybe you should have died in that car along with your mother. I know I couldn't walk around with half a brain.'

'I still have my brain, Barry.'

He laughed. 'How does that work?'

I didn't tell him I was living and walking through a long tunnel and everyone else was far away on either side. I saw Momma dying in the car, my body and hers were so broken up, it looked as if were we sewn into the metal. Matt and Christy being calm on the scene. She's dead, I screamed at them You don't have to go gentle getting her out. Later in the hospital they pointed out the areas where my brain had slowed down. You're not different. You just use slower gears.

The first time I shaved myself, I saw that Joey was gone.

Joey of the white shirts and the Audi car. Joey would magic up a house, an office building from that part of the brain that I couldn't reach anymore. Joey who loved Barbara. Joey who wanted to marry Barbara.

I cut my cheeks with the razor blade.

Barara gave me and Poppa a Christmas present of fruitcake. Instead of icing she put fruit and nuts all jewelled up with apricot jam. She said it must be lonely for two men in a house with the woman gone. She put her arms around her chest and told me not to stare at her face.

'Didn't I love you once?' I said.

'Don't be stupid,' she said.

'I could have you back,' I said.

I kissed her on New Year's Eve morning in her shop.

'That's for Auld Lang Synge,' I said.

She put a mint sweet in her mouth and put her hands into pockets.

'You're not the same Joey anymore,' she said.

'You never came to see me in the hospital, Barbara.'

'I was being practical, Joey. I had stopped loving you and a car accident wasn't going to change a thing.'

'Why did you stop?'

She stared at me now. 'It's like I couldn't love you enough. It was like I couldn't feed you enough.'

Barry came looking for me with curled fists. I said hello Barry and he said we need to talk, Joey.

No One came along too, walking ahead of us and we turned into the green lane, past the empty Crowe's house. We stood on the rocks above the bay.

'I would beat you stupid, but you already are,' Barry said.

He stared over at the horizon.

'I kissed her,' I said.

Barry laughed. 'She scalded herself under the shower. She said the smell and the taste of you was like a bad ghost following her. Say you're sorry, Joey. Say you will never do it again.'

I got down on my knees. 'Like an act of contrition?'

'Just say it, Joey. Say I'm sorry. Say I will never do it again and say I'll stop staring at her'.'

I heard his words through my ears but they just turned into pictures and reversed themselves at the same time so I did kiss Barbara again and I did stare at her as much as I wanted and she stared back and she kissed back and there was no Barry to stop anything anymore, and I was at the kitchen back door munching on rashers and toast and Poppa was turning over his land and whistling at the good of the lovely sky above.

'Say it Joey... say it you dumb stupid fuck.'

He hit me. The pain came through my ear and into the middle of my chest. Something roared and I butted my head into Barry's stomach. He staggered then he fell off the rock and onto the sand. He didn't move. I jumped down and saw his head was bleeding. I sat on his arms and body. I put my hands over his nose and mouth. It took a long while, but he died.

No One came over to me and licked my hands and he and I sat for a while to watch the tide as it came back in. The sun was still hot in the sky. I thought of Old Joey. He was dead.

'Mustn't forget to get the soda bread for Poppa,' I told No One.

We walked back up the green lane, past the Crowe's house and all time we were walking I thought that it was so easy to have killed Barry. I looked down at the bright brown shining fur on No One's head, then I looked at the brown and yellow and red leaves that had fallen from the trees, and the dirt ground beneath them, the stones, then a crisp bag, then another dog barking and a man's voice yelling at sheep, then the sound of someone's car and everything was as ordinary as it ever was going to be for Joseph for now and ever after.

IT CAN BE GOOD

Fist punch. Foot kick. Body bang.

'You fuckin' bastards. Call this a cop shop?'

Someone walks close to the opposite side of the door.

'Stay quiet in there!'

Fist punch to the approximate point that voice came through.

Mouth on my side of the door. 'Is that you, you Big Foot Bastard?'

Fist punch on his side of the door.

'Pipe down now.'

I pipe down and my breath sounds hard. Give him a few seconds of thinking he's got me done. Now. *Fucking bastard cops. Wankers hauling me in here.* I can see them shaking their heads, smiling, calling me a sorry bitch, some returned daughter of the isle now all misshapen and foreign with an accent.

I pissed on the side of the road in Turkmenistan in front of a bus of travellers, I yell now. *Do you think being arrested frightens me?* The bus driver whorled his tongue through his broken teeth when I got back on the bus. Other men said things. I didn't understand the language but my new husband dragged me down to my seat and said, 'Why couldn't you hold on to it?'

'I'm a nurse. I know what it does to the pelvic floor and bladder if you hold on.'

An old woman drew her scarf from her mouth and spat at me.

We were on a kind of honeymoon through Central Asia and beyond. We hadn't any rings but Jerry said we could pick up cheap lapis lazuli in this market he had heard of in Herat, in Afghanistan. The bus bumped along the road to the border checks between here and there. Old men tugged at my dress. Young men clicked their tongues. Young women gave me their eyes, dark and watching. I smiled at them. Some of them looked like the girl from the *National Geographic* photo. Jerry said to come on, let's get the next bus. There were more chickens than goats on this new bus. We sat at the back. The hot dust rose up through the window. I was far away from home. I was twenty-two. I was married to a man with a beard and beautiful eyes.

Fist bang from the other side of the door, then the door unlocks and opens.

Big Foot Bastard stands there.

'Hello Sergeant,' I say.

He is joined by Little Miss Nice, a small and round female guard.

'Stop yelling your useless stories at the top of your voice,' Big Foot Bastard says. 'We don't need to hear about your

Turkmen... sten trip.'

'Never been abroad, Sergeant?'

'I'm just back from Lanzarote,' Little Miss Nice says. 'I'm all brown from there.'

Big Foot Bastard holds up his hand. 'You were arrested for being drunk and abusive in Knocknacarra.'

'I was pushed.'

'Witnesses say you mis-stepped.'

'Mis-stepped? Whoever says that word in real language? I was pushed by my sister's boyfriend, and wankers with their phones filmed me. You didn't arrest them did, you?'

The ground spins below my feet but I haul myself upright against the faint. I think of Jerry. Jerry dead and on the bed. The rhyme won't leave me now.

'You don't understand,' I say.

'If you stay quiet, I can bring you a cup of tea,' Little Miss Nice offers.

'I'm grieving,' I say.

Big Foot Bastard looks at me. 'Over what?'

I say nothing.

Big Foot Bastard says, 'You're going to have to sober up now, aren't you?'

'Go fuck yourself,' I say sweetly and I think of Jerry smiling at me. Go fuck yourself, we had sung to each other across hotel rooms and finally in our home in Eastwood, Sydney, Australia until he was dead in a bed.

Fist bang on the door. *I've been in better cop shops than this. I was in Darlinghurst with all the prozzies and junkies, and they were the cops. You know you always made sure to have someone with you, when you called the cops. The rapes they got up to, otherwise.*

Jerry said, 'You idiot, letting them near you.'

Our flat had been burgled so I called the cops. They came into our sitting room and picked up things. One of them picked up me.

Jerry cried next to me in the hospital. I was open-raw and bloody. I screamed go fuck yourself at him. Later he said he couldn't break my barriers, he couldn't climb my walls, and I was failing to see his own pain. I said what pain? He said, you know. I said the pain of some bastard's dick inside you? That pain? The pain of some wanker's fist against your throat so you don't scream? That pain?

Kick the door. Kick. Kick. Kick.

A kick from outside. 'Shut up in there!'

I think of Jerry's dead white face on the bed. His teeth are white too. His eyes and mouth are open as if he has just yawned.

'Jerry,' I say and he says nothing.

Sudden Adult Death Syndrome. It is as common as a cot death.

Big Foot Bastard tells Little Miss Nice to return to her station.

He stands in the doorway. 'You're quite the article,' he says. Then locks me in.

I punch the cell door. I kick and kick and kick.

I was pushed!

I hurt my face but stood up fast, fists tight. A crowd was around me.

'She's drunk. She's plastered. She fell,' my sister's boy-friend explained.

Someone put his phone to my bloody face. So did a girl dressed like a student. I tore her phone from her hands and threw it on the ground. She fell to her knees to look for it. She wailed when she realised it was cracked.

More phones clicked and clacked.

'Fuckers,' I screamed. 'Wankers. Pricks with phones.'

'The language out of you,' an old woman shouted.

'Fuck you,' I told her.

Ambulance men came first. I shoved one of my fists into one of their faces. The cops arrived. A big one of them got out of the Garda car and told me to behave myself. I spat and buzzed with swear words. *Prick cop. Wanker. Fucking tyrant. Bastard shit on a stick. Is this how you treat your returned citizens? I fucking emigrated when bastards like that little prick did this country out of our money.*

Jerry dead. Jerry dead in our bed.

Cop on top of me. Cop inside me. Cop grinning from the fridge eating my homemade coffee mousse. He left some and I fed next door's dog with it. He threw it up later and I listened to it hurl and puke, wishing I could hurl and puke the bastard's scum out of me.

Jerry said, 'I think you need more counselling.'

I was brushing my teeth and told him to go fuck himself. I thought I sounded almost better.

I came into the room and he was lying quiet on the bed.

I lay back on my pillow and looked sideways at his eyes.

'What's on the ceiling?' I said.

I touched him and he didn't move. I slapped him and he didn't slap me back. I hit him and his skin just shuddered. I climbed on top of him and yelled into his open face. He didn't do a thing. I shoved my hand onto his heart and I tried to punch through. His body lifted a bit but nothing else.

I cried oh Jesus god oh Christ oh St Anthony oh all the

saints oh Jesus Jesus. His beautiful teeth, his lovely beard and his dark open eyes. When we had made it to as far as the coast of Sri Lanka, we had our lapis lazuli wedding rings and we decided that gold didn't matter at all.

I called the ambulance. The cops came too. I recognised a couple of them. I went berserk and they hauled me in on suspicion of nefarious murder. I laughed madly into their faces. I kicked and kicked and kicked. I punched the cell door.

My sister took me to see the swans in the Claddagh. She said the Spanish Arch Museum didn't know if it was an art gallery or a museum. We stared at the large Galway Hooker suspended from the museum's ceiling. We admired photographs of our ancestors in nineteenth-century Galway. We walked through Shop Street, Quay Street, Cross Street, Mainguard Street. We shopped in the Saturday market and bought vegetarian curry from hipsters. We attended book launches and plays in the Town Hall Theatre. We swam through women buying stuff in Penneys. We went travelling in her car and she patted her steering wheel in time to the song on the radio.

'I was raped once,' I said.

She took her eyes off the road for one second, then put them back on to it again. She whispered, 'Oh, Jesus,' then she drove on beyond Knocknacarra and further to Silver Strand Beach, where there was a line of silver between the sea and the sky. She lit two cigarettes and gave me one. She stared at the sky. A wood pigeon called out from a few trees inland. *Caw caw caw caw-caw* and on until it stopped, then started again. I followed its rhythm in my head while watching little flies alight on dry seaweed. My sister was crying.

I told her all my thoughts were snapped into pieces and they shifted places in my head. Now there, now here. Now Jerry, now the cop. Now Jerry dead, now me still alive.

I lay back on the warm dry sand. The waves came in and out close to my feet.

The counsellor had told me a long time ago that I would have to string my life back together again, like one of those old dolls with wire running through the gaps in their bodies. Jerry's mother thanked me for loving Jerry. Jerry's father said even though it was a short marriage for me, maybe I'd find another soon enough. My sister said, come home. My parents said we love you.

I worked in a library for a while, glad to whisper instead of talk. Then I moved into Revenue. Head down into a computer. Yes, Sir you owe us tax, Sir. Yes, Madam we live to cream off your hard work. Thank you for your abuse, Sir. I don't mind, Sir. We are coming for your money, Sir.

I found out from Facebook that my rapist cop was getting married. I befriended his wife-to-be and told her about her prospective husband's penis in my vagina. I described it exactly. She said she wanted to FaceTime me. Her face was pretty. She had long hair. She said he said I was lying. She said he said that I was just this mad Irish bitch whose husband died in suspicious circumstances.

I almost laughed. 'You mean curious,' I said.

She ended FaceTime.

Then I met my sister's new boyfriend for the first time over a drink in Tigh Neachtain's.

'Oldest medieval pub in the world,' he said.

I drank vodka and began to cry.

'She's remembering her husband,' my sister said.

'Hasn't he been dead for almost a year?' her boyfriend said.

'You don't forget them that quick,' my sister said.

Her boyfriend nodded, not interested. He was moving in and I was upsetting the scene. I drank more vodka in the guest bedroom. I sang Go fuck yourself at the top of my voice. My sister's boyfriend stalked backwards and forwards in the kitchen downstairs in the morning. He said I'd have to move out. I threw a kitchen chair at his head. I missed.

He said he was calling the guards.

I stood at the front door. *Let them come. I'm ready for them.*

My sister's boyfriend followed me out. I hit him and he hit me back.

Fist punch. Kick. Shoulder shove.

Wanker, fucking bastard.

'Quit that language,' Big Foot Bastard shouts through the door.

'Jerry's dead,' I scream through the door.

I sit down, then I laugh because it is a normal afternoon outside and I am inside a cop station. I laugh because Jerry died after a cop raped me. He died so quietly. I laugh because I told my sister that I am all snapped up into pieces. I laugh because this only ever happens in nightmare fairy tales. I keep on laughing because the tears are coming and I want them nowhere near me. I laugh so hard that I have to kick the door.

Kick. Punch and a shove. *Fuckers, you wanker cops. Let me out*

The door opens and my fists go first, punching through the air. I see cops in their light blue and dark blue uniforms. They stare at me. My toes tense in my sandals. My heels slick in sandal sweat. My sister is standing there. She smiles at me. She is wearing a blue summer dress and looks sun-dirtied and alive.

'Oh God,' I say.

'Let's go home,' she says.

She holds out her hand to me but Big Foot Bastard warns, 'We won't be so lenient next time.'

Little Miss Nice asks me to sign a piece of paper, then gives me back my bag.

'Thank you,' I say.

'It's a pity you won't thank me,' Big Foot Bastard says.

My sister and I walk towards the entrance. The sun is hot coming in through the doorway and onto the floor. My sister squeezes my hand. A man comes up towards us and for a second he looks like Jerry. But he's not. I turn and shout into the cops.

'Motherfuckers!'

The man falls back and my sister laughs. We half-run to her car and she screeches it out of the carpark. We don't talk for ages but we smile and smoke cigarettes. I look out of the passenger window at everyone swimming in Salthill. They look happy. How many are dying, I think, then I think of Jerry all dead and the cops asking what did I smother him with.

I pull down the passenger mirror and look at my eyes.

'That was an afternoon and a half,' my sister says.

She turns on the radio, zooms down her window

'Motherfuckers,' she calls out.

I smile. 'Motherfuckers,' I chime.

I close my eyes. The sun is hot. I can hear people laughing. I open my eyes. I can come back. I can make a new life. My sister's singing is in my head, off-key and lovely. She flicks her cigarette. She laughs and her freckles jump all over her face. She is alive. Her blonde hair spurts out from its topknot. Sweat shines up the tiny creases in her throat.

She says her boyfriend is history. She says stop drinking and get some help.

She says life can be good.

She smiles and repeats. Life can be good. Smiles and repeats.

We stop at Silver Strand, leave the car and walk along the promenade towards the cliff. Tourists walk and talk. A man and his dogs run into the water.

'Look at that,' my sister says and points out a warning sign for dogs to be leashed while on the beach or pay the maximum fine of € 1,904.60.

'All of that for a dog plus sixty cents and nothing for that Aussie bastard cop,' my sister says.

'Come on,' I say and we wander down to the beach. I don't tell her that sometimes I imagine his sweat and his breath, and I imagine punching my two hands into his face until there is only skin left, limp and skull-less, and now I imagine tossing it to the dogs playing by the sea. Here's dinner, dogs.

My sister and I hop and skip amongst the stones beneath the cliff, then we sit and watch tourists and natives walk up along its edge, not minding the official warning sign: Danger. Keep Clear of Cliff. Falling Stones. Someone in a white sunhat leans over and looks down.

'Get back, you idiot,' I shout up at them.

We laugh and wander back over the beach past elderly

sunbathers and swimmers, past a little girl in a green swimsuit splashing wet sand onto her knees. We sit down close by and share a cigarette.

'You can see Clare from here,' my sister says. 'And the Aran Islands.'

'They look like a giant's blue-grey knuckles,' I say.

My sister blows out her smoke and crinkles her eyes in the sun. 'Hmmmm.'

'Thank you, Evie,' I say.

She grabs my hand hard, then kisses it. 'Life can be good. Don't forget. It can be good.'

'It can be good,' I say.

A wood pigeon calls out *Caw-caw, caw-caw...caw.*

It-can-be-good, the wood pigeon calls. *Caw-caw.*

It can be good.

DEAR DYLAN

Dear Dylan,

There you sat in the pub, your face all curled up in smoke and you wanted me to smile. I said my smile was worth more than any of your boy poems. You said I suited the green juice of your poems, that I am the well-behaved sister of your mad girl. Well, I told your mad girl that I wasn't having any of your slobber on my bed and she laughed and said now why would he like your kisses?

You drank from my beer. You asked for a cigarette, lit and God forgive me, but I opened my mouth to inhale you. Pub voices rolled behind our backs and your eyes looked at mine.

'You've been in love with me for years,' you said and stroked a fleck of beer from my chin.

'Years,' I agreed and gazed at your pudgy smile.

I magicked you up, dear Dylan to have this conversation. I went back in time and through all your poems to find you here, perched solid on a bar stool, smelling sour from the previous night and you've known how many times I have thrown your poems against the wall, your dominionless deaths and your Fern Hills.

And you said you didn't mind where I had blown in from because I bought you a beer and gave you a few cigarettes.

'A poet,' you said. 'Really,' you said.

And you sounded like those taunts in my head.

Well, I am just as good as you, Dylan Thomas, and I'll prove it too.

We were sitting in that pub and I told you that not much has changed between our worlds. There's a war at the moment, not exactly World War Three, but it began in Europe too. Stalin and Hitler are dead but there's another version now and the bombs can fly for long stretches by themselves before they obliterate buildings with people in them, and refugees, there are always refugees... and what is the point of life, I asked you.

'I don't know,' you said.

Then Caitlin broke free from her American airman, pushed in between us, grabbed your head and kissed it. You growled, shook her grip off, took her by the neck and forced her to look at me and said,

'Say hello to this poet, my love.'

Caitlin plucked my cigarette and put it in her mouth.

'Cat got your tongue?'

'No, he's got my knee.'

Caitlin's airman sauntered up. 'Can I buy you all a drink?'

He was tall in a white lemonade way, straight-lined with straight lips and straight eyes. He ordered new beers and of course you cajoled a cigarette from him.

'Can't take you anywhere,' Caitlin said with her eyes on me then just as cool she smiled up at her airman who whisked her off to dance. She was all legs and knickers. Dust raised from the pub floor and men watched from their beer glasses. Women too.

You said, 'Let's shuffle forth, you and I.'

'No.'

You gave me that smile that your mother never stopped loving.

Your mother didn't like me, did she? She said what sort of woman are you to gallivant down here with my son and his wife and child absent? I told her that her lovely son and I wander about the bomb sites in London, researching for his film work. My work too.

'She writes a few words here and there, Mam.'

'Does she?' asked your father. 'Have I heard of you?'

'Not likely,' you said.

'Unpublished,' I said.

Your father asked me about my family and you said I was an orphan.

'They drowned together,' you said. 'A lover's knot.'

They hadn't. I told you they had died quite normal deaths, one after the other, one from influenza and the other from a heart attack, five years apart and so far gone from me, I hardly thought of them except in bed at night when sounds from the street made me lonely and afraid, made me a little girl again thinking of death.

You listened to my work and said 'You have good phrasing. Good rhythm here and there, so I suppose you are a poet in your own right.'

'You said something similar to Lynette Roberts, didn't you?'

'When now?'

'I don't know. Maybe when you were late for her wedding.'

I had written something about walking in a field back home. I had used words my parents had said. *The soft stare of a brown mouse in the dried grass. The fox high-stepping it in the top field. A slew of starlings. The sun baking your backbone until your arse is blazing.*

You said my words were too simple. I went too much for the image of the thing rather than the sound. And no girl poet should ever use the word 'arse'. And what about rhyme you said with your put-on accent, your Welsh 'Rrrrrr', I said.

'Too much love in that poetry of yours,' you said. 'A female poet is what you are. You don't have the men's vigour. None of you do, mind.'

I wanted to hit you. You and any other.

'I have bloody vigour,' I said.

You giggled and turned to watch Caitlin dance. I thought this is where I am, in a pub sniping with Dylan Thomas. I thought of all the characters I could have picked and this is him and me.

Then you slyed your gaze back to me.

'So, a lonely cold bed and page for you now, is it?'

'It's a fine bed and a fine page,' I said. 'I have a desk against the window. I see all the crows and cats and dogs.'

You put your head close to mine and I saw your pink scalp beneath your pretty curls.

Your Caitlin told me that you'd smother me in the end. I told your mad girl of that damn attic, that I didn't need any of your dark Welsh wind and running words. I have my own words.

'Cat's got your knee,' you whispered.

My eyelids squeezed themselves as you leaned in and kissed my forehead. The briny, days-old unwashed smell of you. I thought of the colour of your underpants. Probably some colour beyond any other. Your lips big and baby pink and your tongue licked my damp forehead.

'Sherbet.'

I think. I think. I think I need to clutch at your jacket, Dylan, feel its old wool made smooth by you and perhaps your father or someone you might have stolen it from. I need to clutch it. I need to steady my brain from falling into a dark room at the back of my mind after I read your poetry.

I need my own words.

I try to steady the boiling in my head while you watch Caitlin dance among the American broth and brawn.

Bald-headed youngsters with death-crow eyes and muscles in their thighs.

I hear your voice in my head.

'Put that in a poem, mind.'

You smiled with that face your mother loved as I plucked the cigarette from your mouth and put it to the top of your head, then into your mass of curls which flickered up one by one until you were a mass of brilliant flame, my male Medusa.

I've known of the girls you slept with, Dylan. Girls and sad women, rich women and lovers of your words. How they thrill to your rolling 'r's'. Your mad girl told me that it's your arse they want rolling over them. That white blobby flesh slapping and settling into them or just onto them.

'He wants the cuddling type,' she said. 'Not yours. Not really.'

I am shrimp thin. Shrimp hard and brittle. A man clasped my upper arm one night and cooed at how it almost all fit into his fist. How lovely to break you in two, he had whispered and place you back together again, sliver by sliver. I didn't want to sleep with him, and he tightened his fist about my arm. He said it served me right to know how it felt to have your neck and spine cracked to that inch above death.

I ran home to you and your poems.

I invited you; come sleep with me, said the butterfly to the Cherry Blossom tree.

Then I burned you up, Dylan.

Your face lifted into ashes. Your curls frittered into air. Your words shuddered up through my legs and into my heart. Shelf-dust, gas ring, kettle, cups, the very guts of the world seemed to vomit inside your poems. I thought of our bodies lifting upwards in the blast of your words, then falling back down, all the bodies falling, all dying yet never dead.

DOROTHEA IN THE LAND
OF BLACK AND WHITE MEN

The white girl looks over at our table. She is waiting for chowder while her mother waits for fish and chips. I am waiting for the man in front of me to shut up but he keeps talking, so I have decided to put his voice out of my head and look through the window.

There is an Irish street outside. Yellow, pink and blue houses with green trees and old cars, and the sun cuts my eyes.

My lungs give into a long grunt.

Zach freezes. He is more or less European black, a little diluted from North Italian blood. He jokes that he also has Mafia blood. He squeals if he gets a cut finger. He says he will never visit any country of Africa. Not even mine. He is afraid to discover that we shit in holes and cut female genitals by the light of a full moon.

I made him look at me.

You see? Intact.

He laughed and said, *You African Africans.*

The white girl skims her eyes over us and I hold my phone just so she can see that it's state of the art modern, flat and with earphones. Zach skims his fingers over his.

The man in front of me talks and talks. He is a friend of Eugene's. Eugene is from Paris. He is tall, white with light brown hair, the colour of toffee. He smells of aftershave. He makes my nose twitch.

The white girl sips her chowder and chews whatever fish she hooks onto her spoon. She plucks a chip from her mother's plate. The man in front of me raises his voice.

'You are not listening to me.'

I cluck my teeth at him.

'What are you saying then?'

'I am saying that you must respect my religion.'

A black man and a white man jump into a car on Zach's phone screen and there is smoke, bullets, and hot yellow dust.

'I am saying that you must respect my religion.'

The white girl lifts a piece of fish to her mouth, stops and listens.

'Your what?' I say for her benefit, to give her time to put the fish in her mouth and chew.

'My religion... you must respect my religion.'

'What's your name again?' I say out loud and louder.

'Ibrahim,' he says.

There, I tell the white girl in my head. There you heard. I glance over at her and her eyes cross over mine, then over the back of Eugene's head and finally back to her chowder.

'Ib-ra-him,' I recite.

Zach flicks a finger in my direction. It warns me to be responsible with my manner. My mother often said I was too quick to condemn. *Men don't like to be condemned, Dorothea. They like to be loved.*

I watch Zach's finger until it goes back to scrolling Zach's phone.

'Ib-ra-him,' I say again.

Ib-ra-him doesn't like fish. He is disappointed there is no halal lamb or beef on the menu. He eats a salad with plain oil and sprinkled seeds. He has ultra-white teeth, large brown eyes and a scar underneath his left ear. Eugene has known him for six weeks. They are also studying medicine. They like the Irish climate. They don't mind the lack of heat.

Eugene cuts a chunk of fish. He jerks a smile at me. He told me earlier that he was surprised that Zach had such a colourful girl. I looked at him and he went red to the faintest roots of his hair.

'I mean...' he said.

'It is fine, Eugene. I know what you mean.'

Ibrahim would not touch my fingers in greeting.

Zach looks up, puts his fork into his fish, he chews and goes on watching his phone.

Ibrahim sees the crucifix on my neck.

'Are you Christian?'

'A gift from my mother.'

The white girl gets up from her table in search of the toilets. Ibrahim sees that I watch her.

'At least she is not showing her arse,' he says.

'Or her tits,' Eugene offers.

They laugh. Boys.

'Why did you refuse to shake my hand, Ib-ra-him?'

Ibrahim reaches for the saltshaker.

'Why?' I insist.

Ibrahim smiles at Zach's bent head. 'Why... is she so angry?'

Zach glances up. 'I don't know.' He laughs. 'It's a joke between us.'

You are so angry inside, Zach often says. It must be from your mother. My mother on Skype says, *what a lovely boyfriend you have.* I tell her that we don't sleep together. She believes me. The fact that he is Italian Catholic makes her believe me.

'Why?' I insist louder.

Ibrahim looks at me. 'It is not natural for a woman to be as angry as you.'

The white girl has come back from the toilet, picks something from her bag, whispers to her mother, then returns to the toilet.

'Excuse me,' I say and Zach shuffles back his chair to let me out.

The toilet is nautical. Red, white and blue with passages from a novel printed on yellowed paper and framed. I recognise the white man's whale. The white girl stands there and sprays water on her face and wrists. I visit the toilet and listen to her spray.

'Anything hot does this to me,' she explains when I come out. Her face is red and wet and her neck is blotched and pickled pink. I push my fingers through my hair, then I pull out my lipstick from my bag and colour in my lips. She watches and smiles. My anger rumbles.

'You like my lips?'

I like your lips, my first white man said to me. He touched them. *They are like overwrought rubber.*

I lean against the sink. 'You are watching us.'

Her red skin turns redder. 'I'm sorry.'

I put on more lipstick and my lips rubber up red. I smile at the white girl through the mirror and say,

'They look at this and they think we are a moving vagina. That is what makes them so afraid of us.'

Zach shuffles out again to let me in. *You have hooked him well*, my mother whispered on Skype. *He is studying to be a doctor. You are studying to be a doctor. It is a good match. How is it that you have hooked so well without your mother's presence?*

I sit before Ibrahim. 'I've washed my hands. Now you can shake them.'

Ibrahim's eyes stare at my lips.

Zach looks up from his black and white buddy movie on his iPhone. He sees my lips. He licks his.

Eugene also sees my lips.

The white girl watches.

'God gave me my hands, Ibrahim. Don't you like God's creation?'

Ibrahim curls his mouth. 'In my religion we do not touch women who are not ours.'

'Let's not talk too much about religion,' Eugene says. He avoids my lips but they are moving fast on my face, smiling, pouting a little. I chew with careful thought. Some of my lipstick comes away on my fork.

'I am no one's woman,' I say.

'I am trying to be polite,' Ibrahim says. 'You are not.'

'That white girl is watching you,' I say.

Ibrahim looks over at her and she flicks her eyes down to her cup and spoon. Ibrahim curls his mouth again, so I say,

'She is probably thinking, 'We don't need his kind in this country'.'

Eugene sighs hard, 'Let's talk about something else. Zach... Zach?'

Zach nods his head. He is busy with his phone.

I nudge him and I smile, 'What is on that phone?'

'Your mother,' he says and laughs at his joke. He leans forward to Ibrahim and Eugene. 'Dorothea's mother still pounds her own maize even though she could buy packaged flour in the store. She walks barefoot in the house even though Dorothea has bought her expensive slippers. She believes she is old African. Her grandfather was Mau Mau.'

Where is this anger from, my mother asked, *and why does it infest my daughter?*

I shake my head and my crucifix jiggles on my throat.

'In my religion, you are a slave to God,' Ibrahim answers.

'Really, Ib-ra-him?'

Eugene says, 'Perhaps we should not talk about religion.'

The white girl is staring high above our heads and at the sky outside the window but I know she is listening. I want the white girl to see my anger. It is sweet as sugar cane with spikes.

'I am a slave to my God,' Ibrahim says. 'I worship him in my house.'

'Zach,' Eugene says.

'Yes?' Zach looks up, sees Eugene's face then Ibrahim's, then mine.

'You must respect my religion,' Ibrahim says to all of us. 'It is *my* religion.'

I press my crucifix into my neck. 'So is mine.'

So is mine, I think even though it hardly is anymore. My mother loves God enough for both of us, and even Zach goes to his Mass when he is at his home. I keep rosary beads in my underwear drawer. Sometimes I pray but they are strange words and they do not sop up the anger. *Where did it come from,* my mother wailed after the police had carried me home from a house party, *where is her father when he is supposed to be here to beat sense into her?*

A man had me at that party. Slick of spit and aftershave, a kiss then another then something else... no... no... no... we all say, all of the time. Even the white girl would say it. She would be red with heat and anger. Imagine her naked with a man on top. I look over at her. She would break. She would snap. She would be hung on a hook for a man to eat.

Zach does not eat. In bed, he slumbers. In sex, he moves while I lie there. You are so quiet, he says.

'If you visited my house,' Ibrahim says. 'You would cover your face and head to show respect for my religion.'

'Then I will never visit you or your house,' I say. I slap my knife down. The white girl is leaving.

'To show me respect,' Ibrahim insists. 'You will cover yourself if you enter my house.'

The white girl is at the door and smiles goodbye at me. I smile back then I laugh 'Hah!' into Ibrahim's face. He spits out a salad leaf in shock. He puts his hands together, then twists palm against palm. He looks to Zach. Zach blinks.

'Dorothea.'

Eugene holds up his hands. 'Let's stop this religion talk,' he announces.

I watch the white girl and her mother cross the road and enter an electrical repairs shop.

Ibrahim says, 'If you were my woman, you would wear a *burka* in the presence of other men.'

There is silence at our table. *All this anger,* my mother is fond of exclaiming. *Why does it come out of you?*

Zach puts an arm around my shoulders. 'Let us forget religion, Dorothea.'

Ibrahim looks at him. 'Do *you* respect my religion?

'No,' I say for Zach.

'Yes,' Zach says. He squeezes his hand on my far shoulder. There is noise coming from his iPhone. A white man grins at a black man. The black man gets into the car first. He drives the car. The white man shoots bullets from the passenger window. The car wheels spurt up dust and stones. It looks hot in that picture. I can see the sweat drip from the men's faces. I can feel their hands on the steering wheel and on the gun.

'You do not,' I tell Zach.

He glances up, licks his lip, shrugs and mouths my name. *Be quiet,* my mother's voice says in my head. *Be gentle.*

Ibrahim says, 'I do not want to argue.'

I put my elbows on the table.

'When you have a wife, Ibrahim, what will you do with her?'

Eugene pokes a toothpick out of his mouth. 'Respect is important, Dorothea.'

The sun is warm on the restaurant glass. I want to take out my phone and put my earplugs in and dismiss Ibrahim from my head, but he sits there with his face shining in the sun.

'Or maybe you will have two wives, Ibrahim. Or four?'

For months after, I was afraid of pregnancy but nothing happened. I began to choose clothes that gave me hard edges and a smart mouth. Bikinis and shorts, skirts that lifted if I ran or danced, shirts that opened to the top of my breasts.

No one will love you, my mother said.

I was sent to Ireland to study. *Go back to where the priests came from*, my mother told me. I was a visitor. Drunken men came up to me and said *if I say the nigger word, will you hold it against me?*

I said, say the *nigger* word and see.

They drew up their drunken heads and said the word *nigger*.

I spat in their eyes.

Come over in a boat, love?

Looking for a customer, love?

I decreased my number of white lovers once I found Zach. Coffee-milk Zach with an Italian father and Ugandan mother. Zach, who handed me his laptop one day and said check out this movie. He ate an apple in front of me. He said he had been watching me.

All your white boyfriends, he said.

I drank hard on our first night together, just to keep my anger quiet. It got easier the more I shut my voice into a small place in my head.

Ibrahim picks a sunflower seed from his mouth.

'We honour our women,' he says.

'And that's why you erase them,' I say.

Eugene says, 'Dorothea, let's forget religion.'

Zach looks up at me for a few seconds. *This is not good,*

his eyes are saying. I look away from him and out through the window. The white girl and her mother have come out of the electrical repairs shop.

Ibrahim glances at them.

'She needs an arse,' he says.

Eugene laughs. He leans forward on his elbows to see the white girl and her mother cross to the small river canal. They have linked each other's arms. They are talking and smiling.

'Yes, needs an arse,' Eugene laughs again.

The girl carries an electric iron with her free hand. Its flex hangs down and bumps against her knee.

Ibrahim sucks his teeth, then digs a seed from his mouth.

'There,' he says and presses the seed down onto his plate, links his fingers and looks at me.

I hate you, I say in my mind and to his eyes, then I look again for the girl and her mother and I see them disappear around a corner.

'I will Skype my mother tonight,' I tell the men around me.

They say nothing.

I look at their black and white faces and because my hate is so warm, I smile at all their teeth.

WHITE WIFE

The loudspeaker announced the next race as Anna Galvin approached me.

'Would you like to join us for a cup of coffee?'

I glanced at her friends. The black ones raised their noses and the white ones put down their eyes.

The loudspeaker announced. 'On your marks. Get set. Go!'

We had been friends. We had played poker for Lyons tea-bags and Cadbury chocolate. She was wearing new sandals. Her fingers and toes were French manicured.

'Please join us,' she said.

'No, thank you.'

She looked over at the small collection of Masai women seated on their stools near the dog rose bushes.

'Are you happy?'

'Yes.'

'You're not sitting with them?'

'I can see better from here.'

'Where's your husband?'

'In the next race.'

'Is he fast?'

'His mother told me that he can beat a cheetah.'

His mother sat three metres from me, her legs were stretched out in the sun. A small something crawled over her toes and she brushed it off. Then she saw us. She drew her lips back and Anna assumed it was a smile.

Mama Celestine looked at me and I imagined her gone. Not there. Dead, at least.

'Is she kind,' Anna asked.

'She's his mother,' I said.

'So she's biased,' Anna smiled.

I scratched a mosquito bite on my neck.

Mama Celestine spat phlegm in the direction of my feet. I did not look at her screwed-up face with its hate sitting in her skin pores. I looked at my husband stretching to his toes before the next race. He was taller than the white runners. They flexed. He posed. He gleamed.

Mama Celestine raised her voice to cry, 'See my son run. His legs are swords. His skin is blood red. His eyes will take your souls.'

Mama Celestine told me she had her mother's magic. My husband told me not to listen to her madness. He said his iPhone had all the magic anyone needed.

Mama Celestine had been her husband's fourth and final wife. She gave him five sons.

'You were blessed among women,' I told her.

One son was killed by a lioness. Another son was knifed

to death outside a club in Nairobi. Her third son went away and refused to return. A fourth son died in his second month. Her fifth son gained an agriculture scholarship, excelled in husbandry studies, returned and took control of his father's cattle wealth. His father died soon after.

Mama Celestine was a practical person and insisted that now there must be a wife for her best son.

He met me in an art gallery in Nairobi. He was impressed by me and assumed I was an artist. I said I was just the curator's assistant. We went for coffee. Then more. Then drinks. Then bed. I loved his skin. It felt like smooth glass.

Mama Celestine screwed her mouth when I sat in front of her for her blessing.

'White,' she said. Not even 'mzungu' which would have sounded polite. 'White,' she said. And spat.

Anna said. 'I see your husband.'

Koinet. The tall one. He dressed like a warrior although he had never killed a lion. The elders had accepted that lions were scarce and there was more glory in killing a poacher these days. Koinet had killed three so far.

Koinet took off his shuka to reveal his Liverpool Football shorts.

'On your marks. Get set. Go!'

I saw his legs pound. I had knuckled his muscles last night.

Koinet ran. He lifted one leg and flew over the first hurdle. Another runner, a white man, pushed forward.

'Steady, Koinet,' I whispered. Mama Celestine stared at her son. He had dropped to second.

Everyone else was screaming. Anna Galvin stood on her tiptoes.

'Your Koinet is gaining now.'

Flags waved and wine bottles popped. The white runner was really honey-brown and he was fast. He glanced back once at Koinet who was thundering the ground.

'Steady, Koinet.'

'Imagine them as poachers,' I had whispered last night as we lay together. I put my hand on his heart and he picked off my fingers one by one and held them in the air to sniff.

'Cow's milk or goat's urine?'

'Neither' I said.

My hands had roughened over the past three years. Thin scars crisscrossed the backs and blisters bubbled, then popped on the palms. Once on a visit home to London, my mother cried into them.

'Can't you get a manicure *anywhere*?'

Three years and no child. Mama Celestine was not happy. She told her son that I was killing his penis. Koinet was not superstitious. He had a clear and straight mind. He was interested in the climate and preserving the wildlife. When he was not overseeing his own cattle, he ran a farm for a Chinese businessman, who once assaulted me, quite amused that his right-hand man had a white wife.

Mama Celestine warned me that if I had a slit-eyed child, I would be cast out. There was no child and Mama Celestine said to her son,

'What can you expect from one that is not cut. Nothing roots.'

Last night Koinet said, 'My mother says it is time for a second wife.'

The race was short and the white runner won.

Anna said, 'Why don't you come and have a coffee with us?'

'He'll win the next one,' I promised and lied.

I watched him lose the next race and the final relay. He hung from his waist and his thigh muscles shook. Mama Celestine was not happy. She shouted down to her son and he shielded his eyes to look up at her. He shook his head and shrugged his shoulders. His Chinese businessman approached with a water bottle. He had bet money on Koinet. Some hundreds of pounds.

A woman wandered up to Anna. I knew her to see. She had New York chic.

'Anna, you are spending too much time in the sun.'

She said it as if she cared but her eyes were on me. Her name was Jocelyn. She was a lecturer in African and American Literature. She raised her nose at me. I was that kind of white to her.

'Your mother-in-law is unhappy,' Jocelyn noticed.

Mama Celestine prowled but did not come close and Jocelyn raised her voice to call.

'A good day to you, Madam.'

Mama Celestine nodded, then clicked her tongue at me. *Come, come, come.*

I did not come. I stayed still to smell Joycelyn's perfume and admire her long, red nails.

Come, come, come.

'Isn't she angry,' Anna said.

Jocelyn lit a cigarette. 'You must love him very much to live with his Mama,' Jocelyn said.

I wanted to give a reply but nothing came out except 'I love him.'

Jocelyn laughed.

I loved Koinet's white shirt on his black skin in the art gallery in Nairobi. I loved his protectiveness. He said he loved my mind because it agreed with his and I told him how wonderful to travel nomadic across the Serengeti.

But Mama Celestine cried on our wedding day. 'She is too thin. She has too many bones. She is not a Masai woman.'

Mama Celestine told me since I was not cut I was not a good wife. I would look at other men.

'You are his white wife only.'

Last night, Koinet said a second wife would be a good investment for him. He needed sons and it would be good for his reputation as a warrior and a man. The elders were whispering. A second wife would ease their worries. I could remain his first wife.

Koinet stood up to stretch his legs and his muscles quivered in the lamplight. I sat and watched his lovely body. I wanted to know why I was here in his hut, hundreds of miles from my Nairobi life, thousands of miles from my older life in London. I thought of ordinary things like running up my parents' staircase, the sun on their green garden, raspberry trifle with custard and cream.

I thought *my love. My love.* I wanted to laugh. I fell back to our bed and gazed at the apex of our hut. Things rustled in between its cracks. Tiny insects with watchful eyes. Mama Celestine's eyes.

'Look at my legs,' Koinet said.

He slapped each thigh and posed like a statue that may have been in the gallery where I first met him. I sat up and put my arms about his knees. I kissed each one then breathed over the hairs on his calves. *Lose*, I breathed. *Lose.*

Mama Celestine screamed curses into my face. Anna and Jocelyn said goodbye and rushed off to their friends who watched from their deck chairs, holding their martini, gin and wine glasses. The sun was beginning to die. Mama Celestine said that her son had to hide from his shame. She turned to the other women from the shamba.

'She has poisoned his legs.'

I walked on but Mama Celestine held onto my arm. I looked down at her small, bald head, at her long earlobes and her bead necklaces that jostled about her neck. Hate fitted like a large marshmallow in my mouth. I walked faster but she kept up. She called on her ancestors to get rid of me. Her thin left elbow knifed my ribs.

The road to our shamba curved about a gully of rock and small thorn bushes. I saw the heads of our huts. There was smoke from fires and goat bells tinkled. I thought I can leave him. I can walk to Anna's house in the school compound. I can sit at a real table, drink tea instead of milk or cattle blood. I can put away my love because it is nothing and later I can walk in the midst of modern Nairobi, have a cappuccino, tell my mother that I want to come home, enter a British Airways plane and lift off...

...there was a bird cry and a small cloud of smoke which turned out to be road dust and I saw Mama Celestine lying in the gully. She lay eyes open and still moving. I thought she must have twisted on her feet and her head had struck a small rock that lay next to the roots of a thorn bush. I had heard her bald head crack from a long distance. Her blood seeped out onto the dust and roots. I stood and wondered at her fall. I could hear the chattering from the other women, not visible but coming. Mama Celestine murmured her son's name. Her little heels stuck up and over the gully's edge. Far back in my mind I tried to see what had happened.

The other women turned the curve and saw what had happened.

They hit me and hit me. The blows were far away for a while and I laughed through my own blood. All the greenness of my parents' garden filled my mind. My teeth broke apart and I curled like a baby under the blows.

SOMETHING

He drove fast, one elbow out the driver's window, his jacket off and his shirt sleeves rolled up. Her eyes were closed and she was dreaming of adventure. He began to smoke as he steered the car towards Carrauntoohil. She opened her eyes and gazed across his arms to the sea at the edge of the cliffs. The sky had peeled itself back to its original colour; a blue so pale that it was almost invisible.

'I can see the moon,' she said.

He didn't look. The grass verge dipped and cornered against the car.

'Jesus,' he whispered.

She rested her hand on the back of his neck. His neat hair bristled into her finger-tips.

The car bumped and went faster. It passed stone walls. She rose a little to watch the sea. She wasn't all that sure about the honeymoon. It made her sick, all this love.

He drove fast. His knuckles gripped the steering wheel but now and again they released, and the palm of his hand arabesqued into a left-hand corner turn.

The sea blistered with white sun. A liquid desert, she thought. Then she said, 'I could paint that.' She leaned her face against his shoulder.

'If we had honeymooned in Paris, I could have shown you Monet's gardens.'

He looked at her and she saw something in his face.

'Well, at least I got you away from your family,' he said.

Something in his face. Something new that made her cold.

She sat back in the wine leather seat. This was her father's car. Her new husband was driving her father's car. It was a temporary wedding present. See Ireland before you see Africa, her father had joked. She rubbed her half-ways fringe from her forehead. Her stomach crinkled on the inside. The middle-line of the road bumped underneath the car. Her husband's fingers gripped the gear hard and wrong.

'Soothe it back,' she told him.

And he looked at her as if he hated her.

She sat back into her seat and a slight, unrecognisable fear sat with her. Her vison blurred and pain tightened in her left eye, yet she focussed on the middle line of the road. She wanted to grasp it and fly back with it to the very edge of the morning or even to the previous night. What had she done wrong? What had she missed? She thought of her room up-stairs. It's desk, its books and its pencils and the many faces and heads that she had drawn onto brown paper bags from the shop. Socrates and Beckett.

She tried to see something she had not seen before but she could not see it and after a while, she decided that she had imagined it. It was tiredness. It was relief. It was a headache. It was nothing. This was the start of her honeymoon. It was nothing.

Later she almost drowned off the Isle of Capri. It had been a surprise to almost die. A shock of sunny water and her lungs burned bright hot in her chest. She walked back to the beach and her husband was there, seated at an umbrellaed table with another couple. She stood dripping in their vision. Her husband offered her a Coke. Everything was quiet in her head. She was still on her honeymoon and she knew she had made a mistake. The world crawled around her. People in other lives. She drank her Coke and sat opposite the other newly-married couple. Also Irish and it had being Christopher's idea to pal up with them. Greta's head split with sounds and colours. Her husband wore his black glasses. The other honeymoon couple were delighted with the view of the sea.

The sea was flat, Greta thought. Flat like her husband's face.

In Rome, he hit her. A crack across the face in the Cape d'Africa pensionné.

'Christopher, let's have a day to only ourselves.'

He hit her then and as she patted her bruises with cold water, she studied her marriage from the corner of her eye. Her marriage was a mistake. She pressed the edges of her bruise then applied make-up until it almost disappeared. Things looked good when they could disappear. She breathed in and smiled and when she went out into the bedroom, Christopher was very sorry. He nearly cried. He said it was the sun heating up his brain.

'Maybe we should forget Africa, then,' she said.

He swallowed as he looked at her.

'We could try somewhere else,' she added.

Africa had been her idea. That continent like a club you could hold in your hand. She liked the imagined feel of it. The roughness of its coastline against the edges of her fingers. She touched her bruise.

'You look fine,' Christopher said. He looked pleased.

Another idea had been New Zealand or even Canada but Christopher wanted Africa once he realised how far it slipped down the globe. He was delighted at the deserts and the misleading thin rim of jungles. He heard a priest talk at Mass about Nigeria. He told Greta that Africa was where he wanted to go as well. Two years. Two years of giving yourself in the service of others.

There was something in the way he said that. Something that Greta noticed as a small lie but she told herself that it didn't matter. Her stomach was hungry for something she could not actually see. Adventure, she decided. She packed her art things, her books and her clothes. Her sister Jessie watched her from the corner of her bed.

'I don't think he's good,' she said.

Greta fixed on a hat then pulled her fringe out from underneath the brim. She was going to live in this marriage, she decided. Jessie snorted an angry laugh. She looked mean, sitting on the corner of her bed.

'You'll see I'm right, Greta.' She held out her arm. 'He loves giving Chinese burns.'

Later in Rome Greta had practised. *Christopher, I need new sandals because my toes are hot and tight in my shoes.*

He almost bought them for her.

The shoe-salesman sat on his haunches and lifted Greta's foot to ease the sandal over it but he could not tighten the strap over her high arches. He shoved and stretched the raffia strap to the very tip of the buckle. Greta watched him sweat. Christopher sat nearby, tickling his fingers on the fake leather seats. He had the money. Her money in his wallet. He had said it was better this way. Everything kept together like a real marriage. A bargain between them. The shoe-salesman rubbed his forehead. He held up his hands to say,

'No good.'

Christopher stood up. 'That's it then.'

Greta looked at the shoe shelves. There were so many.

'A different strap,' she told the salesman and he was on his feet to find something to fit the customer's curious high instep. He had not seen such an instep before, he said in his precise English. He ran his fingers over the leather and straw shoes. She watched him milk romance out of the gesture. He had black hair and a crisp shirt but his sweat had made his face wet. He was anxious to choose the correct sandal for her foot. He was anxious to sell.

Greta smiled at him.

Christopher said, 'Let's go.'

She said no to begin with. She concentrated on keeping her stomach tight and imagined that her feet were anchored inside the shop floor. He would not and could not move her. He lifted her up instead. The salesman turned and watched them go. Greta turned and said goodbye as her husband steered her out into the street.

The sun blasted down and the smell of urine followed them.

Young men in pressed trousers with their hate hidden behind zips and buttons. She saw a few turn face towards certain walls and then urinate. Children played with dolls and cars. Nuns sidestepped and Christopher said nothing until they arrived back at the pensionné.

He said she would have to make do with the shoes she had.

'I'm not made of money.'

That was what marriage was. A bargain and an adventure for life.

Greta sat on the edge of the bed.

'My money too,' she insisted.

He didn't hit her and she thought perhaps everything will be fine.

He whistled as he fixed his tie.

All for dinner this evening with the other honeymooning couple.

If the other wife took out a cigarette, the other husband rushed to light it. If she needed wine, he ordered it. If she turned her face, he snatched at her lips with his mouth.

The other husband, Greta thought.

Another husband, she wondered.

Her husband had been so lovely once and now as he walked about their room, she heard the silence climb out from the walls and her armpits grew wet and her stomach slicked.

Something.

She had to find something to say to him.

'Something,' she whispered.

'What?' he said.

His eyes were black and shining in his head.

'What something?'

'Nothing,' she said.

She never told him that she had nearly drowned off the Isle of Capri.

LIFE OR THEATRE

Grossmama died today. She waited until the nurse left the room, then she threw herself from the window to the courtyard below. I ran to look at her body. Her head lay in blood and her legs had snapped; her nightgown ruffled as far as her knees. The sun was hot enough to make her blood smell. Grosspapa returned from his walk, saw Grossmama and said nothing. He lit his pipe, once they had taken her away, while I waited in my room for my own madness to calm.

Dear God, just let me not go mad.

Grosspapa said, 'Well, she did it and that one in her room will no doubt self-murder now.'

Later he complained that if we had not left that American woman Moore's beautiful *l'Ermitage,* this would never have happened. You even painted that woman. She liked having your grandmother and me. We were her Prussian guests and she bought our jewels! But you... you, Charlotte, made us move and now look at what has happened!

Papa and Paula sent a letter. They said they would do everything to help and lead me on the right path. *Your maternal line has degenerated, but your father's is made of vigorous stock. Our sympathies**. Over the days, I sat on my bed and looked through my window. Grosspapa went for many walks. My mind was blank white, hot white. From my bed, I imagined how my foot would feel on the window's ledge, the scratch of wood on my instep. I would have to crouch a little, hold my breath, catch my breath, then fall. I imagined the slam of my body on the hard ground. My teeth would jump from their gums! I concentrated on my head, how it would bounce just a little then settle back, my eyes open... I stood on the window ledge. I had very good balance, yet it would have been so easy, natural... after all, what does one do when there is no hope left?

Grandmother did it. Mother did it. Mother's sister, my young aunt Charlotte walked into a lake. We all did it, I told myself as I balanced there, then I noticed the bright sun on my toenails, and I thought of my old lover... my stepmother's lover... Alfred Wolfson. I remembered his body, his eyes, his glasses.

If I do not kill myself, Alfred... What will I do instead?

'I have to do something, Grosspapa.'

'Kill yourself. It is what all the others did.'

ALL GERMAN NATIONALS ARE ORDERED TO LEAVE THE CITY OF NICE WITHOUT DELAY and Grosspapa and I board a train for Gurs, an internment camp in the Pyrenees. I sit on the floorboards and sketch while people cry, sleep, smoke or stare at me as I sketch. Everyone's head joggles in time with the train. Joggle... joggle... joggle. Here come the German spies...joggle... joggle... French kids scream in through the carriage walls... there they go, the German spies... joggle... joggle...

The French camp commandment tells us we are very welcome to Gurs and must stay here until further notice.

Gurs is a place in hell. There had been rumours of cottages with individual gardens but there are only barracks of German women. German Jews sleep in beds next to German Nazis. Communists drag buckets of water alongside Fascists and the French commandment searches for the pretty girls at night, and one by one each night they return with something to eat.

There is sex here, but I tuck myself into my own corner and I keep away. Sex is such an animal thing in this place — how one body fits under or over another. When I loved *you*, Alfred, *you* complained that I did not move. Did we love each other, Alfred? *Oh God, don't let me go mad.*

There are artists here. They sketch women at the water taps, women at birth, women sharing their coffee. I sketch Grandmother's body, then I sketch my mother dead beneath her window in Berlin. It is easy to see how her body would lie there since she was Grandmother's daughter and they had the same body, the same death.

There are rats here. Sweat, tears and filth. A few women have killed themselves, so tired of living in this world

I cannot find meaning, Alfred. There is only me remaining. Why live for only me?

There has been a Franco-German armistice. Germans are no longer to be imprisoned in Gurs. Are you Aryan? Well, how lovely for you! Are you Jewish? Well. Have you a permit to reside in the Vichy zone? Have you an exit visa to leave France? A transit permit to Spain perhaps? Papers for another country? No? Well, the Third Reich would like you back, perhaps not now, not on demand but soon and until you find yourself on a cattle train back to Germany, you may reside in Nice with your grandfather, Mademoiselle Salomon, since he has a permit, but he needs to be cared for by his dutiful and loving granddaughter, hence you are necessary.

Grosspapa stands in his white nightshirt in a room for the night. I remember his narrow legs and his round knees. Sleep with me, he has suggested. There is no other room since there are so many of us Jews travelling to Nice.

'Lotte, what is more natural when there is nothing else?'

Nothing else. I rearrange the interior of my suitcase, my drawings of you, Alfred, sketches of Grandmother, sketches of other people. I snap it shut and the landlady agrees to give me another room but there is no key and of course something happens in the night, a man with glasses but not you, Alfred. Instead, it is just another German refugee who leans over my bed and everything is horrible so I scream get out. *You* get out!

We are at the end of our world in Nice. 'There is the sea, so jump and drown,' someone says. 'I have tablets,' says another. Everyone's eyes haunt the other. 'We are dead,' they tell each other. 'We have no names anymore. Who are we? What are we? The Nazis are creeping towards us, and we have no permits now, no visas.'

Grosspapa likes his food, and he likes reading the newspapers. He goes for his walks and frequents the cafes. He hears other Jews say, 'We are all dead now. No hope now. The German Reich will demand us all. Have you something to take? Some to spare?'

Self-murdered Jews turn up everywhere and Grosspapa complains that all the invading refugees are squeezing dead any goodwill left towards the Jews. He reminds me to keep our own supplies of Veronal and morphine hidden until we need it.

I tell him that one must put the world back together again. He brushes at me as he would a fly,

'Kill yourself and all this whinging will stop.'

You will strangle him, Grossmama whispered to me the night before she killed herself. *Oh, he has such blue eyes* — I sang Beethoven's 'Ode to Joy' to her and drew her portraits. I told myself that I would keep her alive despite Grosspapa, despite his story about us all... *In this family of yours, every single person commits suicide. Your Grossmama's mother, her sister and her sister's husband... all from a nervous disease... then our own Charlotte drowned herself and after you were born, your mother killed herself...*

...and suddenly I knew. Mother had not died from influenza when I was eight and I knew then why Papa scratched blood from his face when I told him that Mama had promised me she would return as an angel from Heaven. She had promised me this as she lay sick in her bed and now I knew the truth. I knew that there had been so many deaths.

'Grosspapa, I have to do something to stay alive.'

He harrumps and shakes out his paper.

'Grosspapa, I am going to do something wildly crazy because if I don't, I will die.'

'Do what you want. You always do.' He looks at me. 'We are nothing now. Not even our own German selves. What can *you* make out of nothing.'

I travel to Saint-Jean-Cap-Ferrat and I pay for a pink-carpeted room in La Belle Aurore hotel. It is on a hill and overlooks the sea that moves like wet blue paint. I stand in the empty room with my paints and paper.

Alfred told me, *I came out of hell like Orpheus and re-created my life. I lay in the trenches and pretended to be dead.*

*Go into yourself... recreate yourself. Make yourself a new name.**

I will create my own life as if it were on a stage with pictures, fat big pictures, sometimes pages with whole faces, sometimes pictures run into each other like a film reel. I can show footsteps walking on the page, the same figure walking after itself, motion and distance. I can divide up pages to show scenes. I use three colours, red, blue and yellow, with a little white to mix. A three-colour opera after Brecht, with song and music. There will be a **Narrator** moving like a camera in third person. There is a **Prologue,** a **Main Part,** and an **Epilogue**. A Play Bill announces a 'three-coloured *singspiel*'. It takes place between 1913 and 1940 in Germany and in Nice.

The cast for the **Prologue**: Herr and Frau Knarre, their daughters Franziska and Charlotte, Doktor Kann, medical doctor, Charlotte, his daughter and Paulinka Bim Bam, a singer. The **Main Part**: Amadeus Daberlohn — Paulinka's lover and later Charlotte's. Frau Knarre, Herr Knarre and Charlotte Kann. The **Epilogue**: Charlotte Kann and her grandfather, Herr Knarre.

Prologue: Scenes slip sideways, turn vice and versa, compress and elongate. The first Charlotte is Charlotte Knarre. She is eighteen years old and one night she walks out of her family home, walks through the night-lit streets, walks beyond the town and walks into a lake to drown herself. Her sister, Franziska, later becomes an angel who descends from heaven in through a bedroom window in Berlin to soothe her little daughter, Charlotte Kann, whose papa has told her that her mother died from influenza.

Charlotte's mother lying in her bed. The nurse exits via the background. In the foreground is the windowsill. There is Franziska drawing the curtains. She stands inside the right-hand windowpane. There are spots of flowers, yellow and green grass stalks. She jumps to her death.

Frau Knarre spends her days crying, *My little Franziska is dead. First my Charlotte. Now my Franziska.*

Doctor Kann sits in his green-grey chair and tears his nails into his face.

There is something deep and terrible in the house, and it made Franziska sick so she killed herself. It is a large skeleton that follows little Charlotte down the hallway. Its shoulders spread over the tops of the walls. It is monstrous. The hall is red. Charlotte runs from its legs. She runs to the bathroom and sits there on the rim of the bath. She stares at the toilet.

So that is life? That?

A stepmother arrives, Paulinka Bim Bam. A beautiful singer who has a lover in tow, Amadeus Daberlohn, a singing teacher who survived the trenches in the First World War by playing dead amongst the corpses. He lost his voice and his soul. He died then recreated himself.

Charlotte Kann grows up and enters art school in 1936, one of the very few Jews allowed, years before the school was completely cleansed. The teachers insist on strong Art. Third Reich approved male nudes with upstanding musculature, yet Charlotte usurps them and sets their bodies to Mozart's 'The Magic Flute'. She paints a girl in a red dress dancing in the manner of Degas's ballerina and the male nudes flow and bend in homage to Matisse.

Main Part: Charlotte Kahn lies under her lover, Amadeus Daberlohn, her leg raised behind his back. They are surrounded by hot yellow paint; the sun and the sand, yellow reeds speckled with greens. Their bodies are tanned brown. Amadeus wears sunglasses as he kisses Charlotte. Does he love her or Paulinka?

(**Narrator** — Only necessary images will be used in this play. Tape out Paulinka's eyes and mouth in some scenes and use the reverse side for Frau Knarre and Charlotte. Discard scenes of Daberlohn with drink and other women. Secure transparent tracing sheets over the paintings with explanatory texts for the reader. Remember Kathe Kollwitz's *Woman with Dead Child* — how she used the whole page! Her crossed knees touched the edges. Her shoulders enclosed the dead child's face. Express like Munch and Klimt!)

Paulinka sings Bach... *I go with joy toward Death and my rest*. Then Charlotte's own drawings of *Death and the Maiden*, music by Shubert... *Death and the Maiden — that's the two of us*, Daberlohn tells Charlotte, and she thinks that if he is

Death, she can love Death and she does not have to kill herself like her ancestors.

Then Kristallnacht. *Perish Judea! Grab everything you can.* Black outlined in grey, green and red. Some are on the ground having been kicked there. Swathes of red swastika flags flutter from faceless windows. A bonfire in the middle. Books, clothes. No people yet.

Sounds of Germany 'Deutschland über Alles'... the Nazis' Horst-Wessel-Lied. Ha! And a whole page of soldiers, tight as sardines in a tin, one holds a swastika flag but reversed! and their noses — why let us make them into moustaches. Let us all laugh at the funny moustached men.

Epilogue: Herr Kann and Paulinka send Charlotte to her grandparents in Nice where Grossmama is depressed and wants to die. Charlotte sings Beethoven's 'Ode to Joy' to the old woman. Swathes of brown, grey, green and blue elongate the two bodies that hold onto each other. Charlotte begs her grandmother to remain alive.

(Narrator — The paintings in the Epilogue either fill a page or are barely drawn and there are scenes in which the character Charlotte Kann cannot bear to exist until it is too late, and she stands over her grandmother's body, blood from the old woman's head, one leg hidden beneath her body and the other, its foot caught on the window ledge from which she jumped. Technical perspective does not matter as much as the death and horror in this life. Herr Knarre moves into his dead wife's bed.)

Dear God, please let me not go mad.

I present myself to the authorities because I am a Jew. They put me on a bus but at the last minute a gendarme orders me to get out.

Leave right now. Leave fast, Mademoiselle, and don't come back. Stay at home.

Perhaps he thinks I am too German looking, too red-cheeked to be a Jew or perhaps he is a kind man.

Madame Pécher, my landlady, brings me rutabaga soup each evening and tries not to step on my paintings. She mentions that she has a hidden flat if I ever...?

'There is Grosspapa in Nice,' I explain. 'He keeps reminding me that I am his caretaker; that I only have a French visa because of him.'

I paint Herr Knarre's (Grosspapa's) words and his numerous faces in red paint as he tells his granddaughter, Charlotte Kann, her family's history of female suicide.

(**Narrator** — *Suddenly she knew.*)

...that monstrous skeleton and what he has done to my mother, to the first Charlotte, and now he demands I return to Nice, or he will report me. I laugh at him during one of my visits. What, do the Nazis work for them? He is a small, scraggy man who has forgotten that he has no tobacco to refill his pipe and I won't buy him any.

The newspapers report that the Vichy Prime Minister has told the German Commissar: '...the only Jews we have are your Jews.' I have not heard from my father or my stepmother. I finish my singspiel here in Saint-Jean-Cap-Ferrat, the last painting is of a woman bronzed in the sun, painted against the blue sea and sky. She sits atop a cliff. Her canvass is transparent and the sea flows through it. Blue, fast, short strokes of paint but the top right-hand corner remains unfinished, leaving a blue upturned face in silhouette. The woman wears a green bathing suit. Her skin is made from red and brown paint, and she is beginning a painting, this painting. The words LEBEN ODER THEATER? are painted on her back. Life or Theatre?

Yet in this Life Grosspapa will not leave me alone.

'Is it not natural that we are able to comfort each other?'

My skin crawls hot red. I am still alive. Why am I still alive when they are all dead?

This old man has killed so much. If they were all still alive, would they kill him now as he eats his breakfast by the window?

'This is a good omelette, Lotte.'

I sit opposite him with my paper and paintbrush writing a letter, while he scrapes omelette onto his fork, eats it all then wipes his white moustache clean. He finishes his coffee.

'My hat and coat, Lotte.'

I watch him walk up the street, slowly, slowly up the steep street until he falls to his knees, then forward onto his face. Kind onlookers carry him back and place him in his bed and while he sleeps, I continue with my letter.

Beloved, I put Veronal in Grosspapa's omelette, as well as morphine and some opium. He is dying as I write. He continues to die as I draw him lying there and a voice calls out to me, 'Theatre is dead,'... so I am living.**

*Italics from *Charlotte: A Diary in Pictures* by Charlotte Salomon
**Charlotte Salomon was murdered in Auschwitz, October, 1943

FRAU HITLER

O ops, I've made a mistake.
Cross it out.

I am not Eva B... I am Eva Hitler... and Frau Goebbels is not happy. He gave you roses every day from his garden at the Berghof, Magda, but I have his hand. Herr Goebbels blinks his black eyes and wishes Adi and me much happiness

There are some small cakes to eat and everyone raises their champagne glasses. I hold Adi's to his lips. He dribbles out his bubbles.

I laugh, of course I laugh. 'You silly man. You silly Führer!'
He lifts his grey shaking face and smiles.

We are very happy.

There is bombing outside. Adi told me earlier that our Third Reich is now no bigger than a football pitch and the Russians are a hundred yards away. Dust falls from the ceiling after the shelling. I am happy. Yes, I look at my face. I am happy. I am wearing lipstick for my last day. Adi doesn't like kissing me with lipstick. He said that in these days of war all lipstick is made from cadavers. I don't mind. My lips are a good red. The stars in Hollywood wear this red. Adi told me if we had won this war, I would have been in a Hollywood film of my own life. I can still act seventeen with good make-up and it was only sixteen years ago when I met Adi, when he noticed my legs. What a little moustache, I thought.

Now I tickle Adi's face with the hem of my wedding dress, my black chiffon. I want to dance but the champagne is losing bubbles and the Goebbels are yawning. I dance with one of the boys. He stinks of sweat and his eyes are so young they make me hate him. He stammers that I am beautiful. Everything is too warm and mixed with the odour of sulphured eggs. I expect to smell of almonds when I die.

What a small wedding breakfast and at such an odd time after midnight. Frau Goebbels would not allow her Helga be my bridesmaid. I would have liked to have thrown my bouquet to the girl.

Adi is shaking and mumbling through his piece of wedding cake. He tells me that he has mentioned me in his will. *But darling Adi, how can I spend all your money now?*

The Russians *will not* stop shelling. I think how funny it is that we are living underground and upstairs there is only the Reich Chancellery's garden left to us now. All the parties I could have held as Frau Hitler. My dresses from Paris, my shoes from Italy, the Hollywood directors would kiss my hands and the war becomes something that we can all put away, like a hat bill stuffed into a drawer.

Adi pats my hand and says 'It's good that the cyanide

is fresh.' Then he cries because of that Austrian bitch of his, Blondi. They held open her jaws this morning and cracked the cyanide capsule against her teeth. Herr Goebbels insisted that the dog's death was instant, not a struggle, bark or whimper.

'It is like going to sleep,' he assured me.

And I have tried it twice already.

Adi wants to sleep, so I leave him and walk down the corridor. I am not wearing my best shoes yet, so I don't mind too much that they are wet from the ground water. Usually it pumps out perfectly but these days things are different and now the dust from the ceiling mixes with the water to make tiny streams of mud. I wander up into the Vorbunker and ask the Goebbels if I may take the children above with me for some fresh air.

They stare at me and I wait until one of them has to say it.

'Thank you... Frau Hitler,' Goebbels says.

Frau Goebbels sits very straight but I wait for her too.

'It is kind of you... Frau Hitler.'

The eldest, Helga, calls her siblings together. All 'Hs' after Hitler. They run ahead and Adi's secretary, Traudl Junge, decides that she will join me for a cigarette. We link arms and walk like sisters up the steps and into the garden. The children merely walk about while Fraulein Junge and I smoke our cigarettes. It is quiet.

'They are almost here, Frau Hitler.'

'What would they do, Fraulein Junge, if they came upon us now?'

'They would rape us, then kill us.'

'Oh, I am sure my skin must look so dry in this light.'

'No Frau Hitler. You are beautiful.'

'And I am not afraid to die. I am not afraid of anything I have done. Are you Fraulein Junge?'

'I type letters, Frau Hitler.'

'And I love the Führer.'

'You could live, Frau Hitler.'

'And do what after being raped by the Russians? Disappear? I might as well die.'

Fraulein Junge lights one of her last three cigarettes and offers it to me. I watch Helga walk about in a circle while she gazes up at the sky. I could tell her not to bother. It is just floating rubble dust and shell-smoke, but I look up also and remember the lovely days at the Berghof when all of us were happy, when British *Homes and Gardens* magazine could only marvel at Adi's talent with interior design. The wood panelled dining room, the magnificent window in the Great Hall which could be lowered into the wall if our guests wanted more air, and I made such movies there of Goering, Ribbentrop, Bormann, Speer, my lovely sisters — oh our festive days on the balcony and even Mr Lloyd George was surprised by Adi's talent. What a pity the war came after that.

Fraulein Junge says, 'You could pretend to be no one, Frau Hitler.'

'But I am Frau Hitler. I have always been Frau Hitler and I have never been afraid. When Henriette von Schirach arrived in Berghof, desperate to speak with the Führer, remember her, Fraulein? We were having drinks in the Great Hall and Henriette von Schirach sat on one side of the Führer and I sat on the other. "My two favourite girls," he said. Then he asked Frau von Schirach had she enjoyed her recent holiday in Amsterdam. She said, "No, my Führer, I have not." She said she had seen such a distressing thing outside her hotel room,

Dutch Jewish women being herded together then marched off
to a transport lorry. The Führer said in a stone-calm voice,
"We are at war, Frau von Schirach." She didn't stop there. She
told a silly story about being taken to a little school and in its
little classroom laid out on little yellow tables were so many
pieces of jewellery, worn wedding rings, silver table cutlery,
pearls and diamond earrings. She said they had been taken
from those women and now were for sale for a pittance. She
bought a few things, I think. "They were human beings, Mein
Führer," she said. "I cannot believe you accept this. Oh my
Führer, what does it all mean for Germany?" I watched my
husband's face, Fraulein Junge. I watched it carefully. I knew
everyone was frightened to say anything, but I was not, so I
looked at that silly woman and I said, "But *we* are the better
human beings, Frau von Schirach." She and her husband ran
away after that... not happily ever after I think,' I say, then
look towards the children to see Helga still watching the sky.

'Your neck will go to sleep, Helga,' I call. She turns to
look at me. She has not managed to address me as Frau Hitler
yet. I am still Eva. She has such a long stare. If she grows up,
she might be friendless.

The children's favourite man, Herr Misch, Mish the Fish
they call him, has now come up to the garden and says we
must all go down again.

'The End,' I laugh to Fraulein Junge.

We gather the children and we go back into the
Vorbrunker. I kiss each one of the children goodbye, Helga
especially but her stare is not what I want to see.

'Give me a kiss for Uncle Adolf.'

She kisses me and I pinch her for that stare.

Then I'm off through the Vorbrunker, down the stairs

and into the Führerbrunker. I hear 'Frau Hitler' everywhere I go and I imagine I am in Hollywood making a grand entrance for my first scene. Of course Adi is too old and will be too busy to play himself but perhaps Tyrone Power or Clark Gable. *Don't look at the dark walls, Eva. Don't smell the fear, the sweat, the overflowing sewage from the cloakrooms. No, walk head up and purposeful past the drinking S.S guards.* They applaud my walk, then extend a drink and I swallow brandy glass after glass until I don't mind being kissed by them, pawed by them. One or two call me *bitch* but why should I care now. I bite the lips of one and I spit on another. They laugh after me. *Bitch. We loved Hitler's dog more than you.*

A mad woman runs up to me. Her eyes are red and she holds a handkerchief to wipe her nose. *I stand as Greta Garbo stood as Queen Christina of Sweden.* The Hollywood camera is on Frau Goebbels face first.

'Dear Frau Hitler, make him change his mind.'

The camera slowly rises onto mine.

'Dear Frau Goebbels, no.'

I change into my last dress. It is Adi's favourite. Black with red roses on the neckline. I put on some lipstick and I brush my hair. I spend a little time tidying my room even though I know the Russians will desecrate it and I tear up family photographs into tiny pieces. It is as if they exist in another part of the world. Papa. Mama, Gretl and Ilse... how will they learn I am dead? How will they learn I have become Frau Hitler?

I smile and say goodbye to each one of Adi's handsome personal S.S guards. They bow to me. Dust falls from the ceiling and Herr Goebbels salutes. Frau Goebbels blubbers on her knees at the entrance to Adi's study but he shouts for someone to take her away, then shuts the door.

There is just silence except for the whine of the air pumped into the room.

'It's very untidy,' I tell Adi.

He is so bent and his nose is running onto his moustache and he looks like, God no, Charlie Chaplin. I tell him to straighten up. *Be Clark Gable, Adi and no, I do not want to sit yet because I do not know how I want to sit. Herr Misch has told me that he will kill my dogs afterwards. Poor little Negus and Stasi and he will kill them gently, he said.*

Adi gestures towards the couch.

I laugh and say, 'Adi, I don't know if I want to die now.'

The Russians would have a field day with me, you said. Look what they have done with Mussolini's mistress, and you are my wife!

I decide to sit with my legs up and place my shoes under the couch.

Adi fiddles with his gun and it shakes as he practises placing it in his mouth. *Bite down on the cyanide pill and pull the trigger at the same time,* a bunker doctor has advised him. I roll my cyanide pill between my fingers. It glistens because my hands are sweating.

'Will it taste like marzipan?' I wonder out loud.

The ground above us shakes from artillery shells and bits of ceiling plaster fall on my hair so I have to finger-comb it out. I glance about Adi's study. It is too untidy for any camera but if I had one or if I was in Hollywood, the room would be wood panelled with oriental rugs and cut flowers on the coffee table... and there wouldn't be an ending like this...but I won't even see the Russians coming down the stairs from the Chancellery garden, will I?

Adi is looking at me, waiting for me.

Dear God, now I have finished myself in this little hole and I want to laugh and run back all the way through to the beginning because I can't be dying just yet.

'Bite it. Bite it,' Adi screams at me.

I bite.

Nail polish!

Not marzipan!

HAIL THE GREAT SAMOSA

The Great Samosa has many rules.

Rule 1. Wear Proper Clothes

'Your child's dress is the proper length, Madam,' the air hostess assures the white mother who smiles at this success.

There are so many rules in Malawi and the hostess knows the rules and has lived them all her life.

There are so many rules in Malawi. Our dictator Kamuzu Hastings Banda is a strict Scottish Presbyterian. He shivers at women's uncovered arms, at their legs. No female from the age of seven can show their knees in public. They are banned from wearing trousers or shorts. Fashion magazine models are struck with black paint if they show any illegal skin.

If you walk in bare daylight down main street Zomba, you risk denunciation by any concerned citizen or a passing Young Pioneer.

The Head of the Secret Police is informed.

His children go to Sir Harry's. See his first son sit with a gun in his father's jeep.

See him watch one arrest, two arrests, then more. The White ones shrug. They will survive. The Black ones are temporary.

See his daughter in school. Black and White fawn over her. Keep to her good side and admire her belt, a Louis Vuitton cast-off from her mother. It is not part of the uniform, but English Sir knows his bread is buttered on the one true and real side.

At Lake Nyasa, now Lake Malawi, wear what you want. Bikinis, short skirts and shorts. Display your breasts and arms. All that would see you is the water and the sun and the Chambo.

Yes, spies meander on the lake shore. They are friendly or silent. They are blessed by Kamuzu. They enter your house and if you are Black, you bite inside your face. Bite. Bite. While the spies talk of the weather and how is your husband and your daughter? Or are you considering a return to Paris? I have never been to Paris. Is it as they say? You lie and reply that it is every bit the Eiffel Tower, that yes, summer by the Seine is hot and the tourists are annoying. No, I do not wear Chanel. No, I am not rich. You know what the Chancellor College pays me. That book is Zola's. It is not banned. This is our holiday home. No, it is not *our* summer residence. It belongs to the college. My darling, these gentlemen are here to ask questions, to open our books and look in between the pages, to knock over our plants and amble into the kitchen and sample my Millionaire's

Shortbread. My darling, keep your fists closed. Bite, my darling. Bite.

Gentlemen, the bookshelves are harmless. Gentlemen, my wardrobe is simple. Gentlemen gaze at my arms, my legs. My green bikini. That is Chanel? No, it is Yves Saint Laurent, from three seasons ago. They laugh at the green gold tassels on my hip.

My Darling, bite.

The spies admire the cool clear air of this summer house. The prints of Chekov and Yeats above the mahogany study desk. The spies wonder if they are my gods instead of Kamuzu. They are just men, I answer.

And the woman?

Christina Rossetti.

Where is your daughter?

Swimming.

She will be a champion, one says to the other.

Perhaps Kamuzu will keep his golden eye on her, says the other.

They have been to English Sir's Headmaster's Office. They have read of my daughter's brilliance in the swimming pool. They have often spied me there, cheering her on at local trials. How smooth she looks in the water. Her graceful arms dive like the necks of birds.

How wonderful it must be to have a champion in the family, one spy imagines to the other.

How necessary for a champion to be cherished, the other supposes.

They click their teeth while my darling, you rub your glasses with chamois leather. You are wearing your favourite green shorts and no shirt because of the hot brilliant heat and only this morning at breakfast, you joked that we were twins in colour, and we kissed, and our daughter said she would return later from swimming to eat a piece of my Millionaire's Shortbread.

We watch the open front door but there is only the heat outside while our dog snores from the veranda.

One spy finds a book of mine. He does not like poetry, he says. It is too short, yet it uses up so many pages. Look! He turns it upside down and shakes it out. He laughs. He has large white teeth, pale pink-rose gums and now he reaches into his shirt's top pocket to fetch a toothpick which he places between his teeth, and moves it along his front gums, a short two-headed spear that finds its mark beside each tooth.

I could write poetry, he now tells his companion.

You could not.

I would praise Kamuzu.

You would.

My husband puts his glasses back on and says gentlemen, may we offer you a drink?

The spies now examine the drinks cabinet. They sniff each bottle.

Whiskey?

Irish.

This?

Gin.

This?

Cognac.

This?

Soda water.

A drink, gentlemen?

They catch his enunciation, his fine words sauce their manner now. They declare that I am under review by the great Kamuzu. I have not written one poem in praise of him. Why is this? I am in a dry spell, I tell them. My husband agrees. She is currently suffering from writer's ennui.

The spies curl their lips.

Is that a French excuse?

They are more educated than most.

Despair, my husband says before he thinks.

Despair. My husband takes off his glasses and begins to rub the lenses.

I am enjoying a sabbatical, I announce.

One of the spies continues to watch my husband, the other watches me. His eyes are surrounded in loose skin. His lips are thin. His teeth are yellow.

Why have you only whites on your walls, he asks.

Whites. Chekov, Yeats and Rosetti. White and dead. Safe to grace walls. I could have added Keats, possibly Milton, and yes, Emily Brontë for my time here. Another would add Einstein or Freud or God.

It is just what is there, I answer.

He smiles at my useless lie then looks toward the drinks' cabinet.

Despair, he muses. You should not despair in Kamuzu's country. Despair is for dissidents, revolutionaries, bad people, poets who use too many pages. I will have a cognac, Mister Suleman. My friend will have a…?

Whiskey.

My Darling, we have assumed too much. I watch your fingers tremble as they hold each glass tumbler. The cognac is rich and brown, and he wants it to the brim. His colleague licks his lips as the whiskey also spills over the rim. My Darling, when they exited their car to enter this house, you told me we will weather this and thank our God, Sabine is not here. Thank our God, we are together. Thank our God, we may be lucky. They are dressed in suits. They have no weapons we can see. They just want to ask questions. Thank our God, we have our own minds, and we will not fail each other.

Despair.

The Cognac one smiles after he drinks. Madam, you are not a good citizen of this country. You do not praise our great leader, our Kamuzu. He released us from the English. He made us stand on our own feet. He keeps our hearts clean and strong.

My wife can use those words, my Darling says. He tips the whiskey bottle into the other man's glass. My wife can use your words. Clean and Strong. They are good words. A clean red heart, my Darling says. His eyes scramble with love and fear.

Blood is clean and strong, the Cognac one agrees.

I will write a poem, I say.

It's title? the Cognac presses.

'Kamuzu' to begin with, I say.

A working title for something greater, my husband says.

They finish their drinks, then walk outside to stand on the veranda. The lake is hot blue under the sun. Whiskey glances at my bikini.

A woman should not wear such a thing. It is against Allah.

We are not practising, my husband says.

Whiskey sucks his teeth. Cognac tells him to start their car before he turns to me.

I will inform my supervisor who will inform Kamuzu to

expect a poem from you.

We smile at each other.

I will also mention your daughter's dedication to her swimming. I will mention that there may be medals in her future if God is good.

He looks about as if to see her but there are only the palm trees that align the path down to the lake shore.

Goodbye, Mr Suleman, Mrs Suleman.

Goodbye.

The black shining car drives away. We say nothing. I stare at the palm tree path. I place my hands on my bikini's gold tassels.

Kamuzu is adamant that Malawians must be modest in their public dress and to be anything other is to insult this great man. Pray for him. Pray to that Scottish Presbyterian God that Kamuzu will keep his people's hearts clean, red and strong.

Rule 2. Do Not Speak Against Kamuzu

He is there for life, like any father wants to be for his precious children. Yes, he is temperamental and capricious in his likes and dislikes, but he has so many worries and can trust very few. He killed lions in his youth. He killed English but now he is a political giant, a great man and leader.

If you speak against Kamuzu, how can he trust you? If you, a lecturer in Chancellor College, marry a white woman, is that not a minor betrayal? Is it not like a small stone that embeds itself in Kamuzu's heart? You are diluting your essence, creating beings of half-essence. Kamuzu will accept them, but can you be trusted?

Poets cannot be trusted if they do not speak well of Kamuzu. These words that some disappeared poets have used... *'castrate the lion!'*... *'stand on the edge of Chingwe's Hole, watch the old man throw his enemies down... oh sister, my sister, why do you groan under the old lion's belly?'* Such sacrilege is dealt with most severely. Of course, people disappear but that is their fault. Chingwe's Hole holds nothing but the old way to the bottom of the Rift Valley. Try it and see. If you return, Kamuzu will still be here.

Rule 3. No Television

First, there is the veranda with its red cement floor, its low wall and its white round pillars. There are three windows fitted along the back wall. Look through them and you see the hallway, the way through to the toilet and bathroom and three doors to three bedrooms. I take one for my study since my Darling maintains that the nook beside the fireplace is perfect for his bureau. The middle room is ours and the last room has a long window facing the garden which at least has a view of the horizon and a mountain. She is disgusted that we have returned to Malawi. She had plans to live in Paris. The Sorbonne will still be there, I tell her.

The front door is on the left side of the veranda. Inside there is a settee under the main window also on the left. My husband's bureau is there in that corner, then the fireplace, then the piano that I play now and again and there are two cane chairs complete with jungle printed cushions that we bought from a family returning to England.

There are red and white pouffes made from camel hide and a circular sisal mat lies under the coffee table. There is a music centre beside Hugo's bureau.

There is a large dining table at the far end of the room. It has eight chairs. There is another large window that looks out to the back garden and the washing line. There is a bookshelf that holds Shakespeare's *Collected Works*, a volume of Keats, there is James Baldwin and Langston Hughes and Jean Toomer.

There is no television anywhere, Sabine cried out when we first arrived.

There is a radio.

There is no television. It is a crime to have a television.

Television is against God. It rots your brain and severs your allegiance to Kamuzu. It makes you think that there are better countries than Malawi to live in.

There is France, Sabine cries out and our cook looks up from cutting the carrots. Have you seen what they have done to *Vogue*? Sabine flicks the magazines pages in front of our eyes. Models with blacked out arms and legs. Even visible knees are no longer allowed in public! No shorts or jeans.

She is shocked. Her life is over.

Our cook's name is Helen. She is quiet. She is excellent with 'Madame' and 'Sir'. She irons well. Her cooking is ordinary, and she likes to learn what I can cook. Soon she has French dishes for our dining table. My husband jokes, where did we find you? We all know that answer. She was found for us.

She dusts the bookshelves, handles the books. She never asks questions, but she listens and enters our rooms and my study.

Does Madam need a cup of tea?

I am not thirsty yet, Helen.

She gazes at the poets on my walls.

Does Madam work today?

Yes.

Does Madam work the day I am not here?

Usually.

What does Madam write?

Stories, essays, poems.

Helen smiles. She reaches over to polish a vase and glances at my paper. She says she only got to Standard One but we cannot be certain of that.

Then one day she says you have so many photographs of your friends, your white friends too. You have no photographs of Kamuzu?

I have words with her. I imagine I am white, and I use that accent the whites use. You have no permission to enter my study. It is my study. My domain. You cannot trespass. You only reached Standard One and my vases, my pens and my papers do not need any dusting from you.

She sucks the insides of her lips. Yes Madame.

She fastens her hold on our kitchen. Sabine complains that she no longer feels welcome while she searches the food cupboards for biscuits or cartons of juice. Helen irons our clothes until it is like walking within cardboard. My husband says be careful my love. Be careful with your admonitions.

Helen, less starch please.

Helen, less salt next time.

Helen, the tarte Tatin was unexpectedly hard this evening.

Madam, what is that voice on the radio?

The BBC World Service, Helen.

And that voice, and that voice?

Two tramps, Helen. They are waiting for someone.

Who?

Kamuzu.

Helen is delighted and listens for more but understands very little.

Rule 4. Censorship is Not Censorship

Many visitors to Malawi are surprised at the rules and the certain things that are not allowed to stain our beautiful country.

Women's magazines contain so many images of women's bodies. Swimsuits display legs, arms and sometimes minor regions of the female buttocks. Why is it necessary for European ex-colonialists to show what we already know about the female body? There is a fashion magazine, *Burda*, popular with the white women in this country who like to sew their own clothes and we do not censor the magazine's patterns, merely the images of under-dressed women. See *Rule 1*.

Sabine comes home from Sir Harry Johnson's with a note condemning her lack of respect. She must not leave pool practise in her swimsuit. She must ensure her legs are covered. It is also reported that Sabine has entered Kandodo in her new plaid trousers. Her name was given into the police station and although it is a minor enough offence, if such offences add up to a list, then what is Kamuzu to think of his prized young swimmer? Has she no longer any loyalty to the man who will ensure her path to greatness?

I am my own greatness, Sabine cries.

Ssssh, her father says.

Does it say who informed? No, of course not. It's all eyes and mouth in this country. It makes me want to be with whites all the time. They are so safe, aren't they Maman et Papa, hmm?

She blames her Papa. It's because he is paying you all the money you want. It's because he wants you to teach all the young university men to be architects that will build brilliant buildings for that stupid old man, that worm.

Sabine begins to miss swimming practise and spends time at Zomba Gymkhana Club.

By all means frequent Zomba Gymkhana Club and its cinema. Many films are shown there, and it has caused a little talk amongst new whites that the kissing scenes are shortened or deleted. You do not need to see any more than what Kamuzu has deemed necessary to see. It is obvious what might happen next. European films are notorious for sexual filth while Hindu films respect the Scottish Presbyterian philosophy.

Zomba Gymkana Club caters to both native and non-native Malawians. There is golf, squash and tennis. There are Christmas pantomimes, the latest was the very successful *Ali Baba and the Forty Thieves*.

Sabine explores the golf course. She is regarded as a moneyed girl and the caddy boys grin and say hey, you are beautiful, hey, can you see me, hey, is this what you want, beautiful girl, hey, will you kiss me, beautiful girl or I will kiss you? They encourage her to play golf and she says oh the ball is going to fall into the bushes there and the caddies run to find it. She gives a kiss for each ball found.

Her father cries out that he is in despair.

It is your fault I say. It is your fault we returned here from civilisation.

Rule 5. Spiders are Not Only Insects

All those magnificent buildings for the new Lilongwe, for the improved Blantyre, Kamuzu's new Eton, his crème de la crème, his seedlings for the Secret Police, his minor to his greater spies. They navigate like spiders into each school classroom, business boardroom, housewife's kitchen, a study room and a lecture hall.

Madam Suleman.

Yes?

I glance at the pretty spiders, all correct and perfect in their seats.

Madame, why is Chekov necessary for us?

A trick question and no one would ask it in a less than innocent voice.

He is a great writer who excels at portraying human relationships, I answer.

But he is not our writer, Madam.

No, you will become our writers.

When you consort with spiders, you must watch their legs.

And what is so wonderful about Shakespeare's Sonnets, Madam Suleman?

I laugh because that must be a joke, but the pretty spider does not smile.

They are wonderful because they are beautiful.

Why not one of our poets, Madam? Why not you?

I stand tall by the lectern although my belly sags inside. Is this a new Spider I see before me?

I am not Shakespeare material, I say. And some of our poets displease Kamuzu.

Like whom, Madame Suleman?

The lecture hall is silent. I don't know, I answer.

The pretty spider smiles. If I looked closer, perhaps I would see her Young Pioneer badge.

Mussolini had the black shirts. Hitler, the brown. Kamuzu has the red.

Kamuzu wishes all his citizens to lead productive lives. Such citizens must follow the rules on which our Kamuzu has built this country. It was once known as Nyasaland and under British control. It is ours now.

Yet there remains talk against Kamuzu. It originates from dissatisfied people such as poets and academics, and writers of fiction stories that have no right to exist. These sorts of people seek to destabilize Kamuzu. That is why we have many methods of censorship and defence.

This is why we have the Malawi Congress Party.

This is why we have the Young Pioneers, the Red Shirts.

This is why we have the Police, aka the Secret Police.

This is why we have Zomba Central Prison.

And if people have disappeared, perhaps they have merely lost themselves.

Rule 6. The Greatness of Kamuzu is without Question

Mussolini never slept. Hitler dragged Germany up from its knees. Stalin rearranged an entire people to his specifications. Mao Zedong followed suit.

Kamuzu Hastings Banda is a lion greater than Idi Amin. Kamuzu feeds his cubs from his own plate. He feeds them their own blood.

Rule 7. Do Not Take His Name and Image in Vain

My husband insists I will not disappear if I play by the rules. He insists I will not be like the other poets, Jake Mapenje or Felix Mnthali... He insists that he did not know Kamuzu could lie. He insists we will see Paris again. I laugh for it sounds like his own poetic idea. He insists that it is.

A white family has moved next door. Half-Irish, half-English, three children. The eldest, Livy, likes books. She studies my bookshelves while her mother Hanora and I converse about art, about Florence, London and Paris. Sabine watches the neighbour's daughter pick up a book, read a few lines before taking it from her, suggests they play tennis outside.

They are white, so white. An armour of pale sweat and freckles. They follow the rules to the letter. Livy wants to be a poet.

We have a party to welcome them. We are eager to show that we are modern Muslims. We invite priests, lecturers, doctors, primary school teachers and of course everyone follows the rules. No one speaks of Kamuzu. Helen is in her kitchen. My husband has bought champagne. We toast to new friends.

Oh, the whites are so giving with their smiles, so civil to Helen. The beer is beautiful, the roasted poultry, the fatted cow are laid out along with coffee mousse, raspberry trifle, baklava, nougat, halva, dates, almonds, honey and cardamon.

Oh, the blacks are so welcoming with their smiles, so eager to exist without fear. The beer is beautiful, the guavas are delicious, the roasted pig and spiced and stewed goat, the wine is from South Africa, red and white.

All our children are laughing. All our lives are good.

A priest, a Fr. Roche, announces that he performs magic. May he have someone's wristwatch?

A man I don't know, a friend of a friend, a man on holiday from his car dealership in Blantyre, holds up his watch. A fake Rolex but of such calibre. It possesses a superb bomb-like tick and foils airport customs every time. The watch has Kamuzu's face whose eyes twinkle between ten and two, whose smiling mouth nestles above six.

The Car Dealer man says he trusts a holy man who is also a magician.

The priest wraps the watch in a handkerchief but now he requires a hammer. Sabine brings one from the kitchen. My husband says perhaps magic is not a good game tonight, but Sabine says sssh Daddy, I want to see. The hammer comes down. A crack. A ping of springs.

Fr. Roche smiles at our terror.

Not to worry, he says. These are magic hands.

He says his magic words, waves his magic hand, then uncovers the watch.

It lies in pieces.

Oh poor Samosa, Livy cries. Her father slaps his hand onto her shoulder.

Sabine laughs. Shut up, my husband tells her. Now none of us wants to breathe. The priest's face is sick.

The watch owner screams. Kamuzu. Kamuzu.

I've made a mistake, Fr. Roche says

A mistake? There can be no mistakes! Where is your magic?

Fr. Roche takes a pen from his top shirt pocket to sift through the watch debris.

If it was a real Rolex, he says, it would not break.

It is real, its owner yells. Kamuzu says it is real!

Oh Jesus, Hugo, our new white neighbour whispers above my ear.

Oh Allah, I whisper in return.

But it's just a watch, Livy says. Her father hits the side of her head.

Did I see that, I wonder?

Fr. Roche raises his hands for forgiveness. It was just an accident.

The police come. The Red Shirts come. They take our names. They look at our faces.

How many of you laughed to see the hammer come down?

How many of you cheered to see such fun?

How many whites laughed?

How many blacks cheered?

'What?'

'You insulted our Hastings Banda Kamuzu,' the Redshirt man says. 'You are under arrest.'

'This is crazy talk,' Fr. Roche pleads at all the whites but none of them can help him.

'It's easier if you just say nothing,' my husband advises.

It is a sin to destroy Kamuzu's face. Bad magic, evil voodoo, malignant juju. You will pay for sin. People disappear but there are always reasons. You must understand the reasons.

Livy's mother, Hanora, halts on our veranda.

Will they report on us?

Who?

Spies.

I look at Livy. You are a white, I assure her. A child. 'Samosa' can be nothing more than a mispronunciation, easily rectified. No one heard, Hanora. No one.

Rule 8. Honour Kamuzu

We are preparing for the dictator's visit. Chancellor College erects a podium.

Mrs Suleman, you will recite a poem praising Kamuzu? A question in a phrase.

I sit in my study and play with my pencils. Sabine enters. She smells of the school's swimming pool. Helen follows her. You cannot be here, she says. Your mother is working.

I put my hand over my blank paper. I am working.

My darling daughter pirouettes on the red concrete floor. I gaze on her face, her limbs, her feet, and fingers. My eyes cut her out as if she were a paper doll. Cut her out and put her in my mind's eye. Free and beautiful. She dances out of my study.

Now you can work, Helen says and leaves.

Tell me, how does the lion Kamuzu eat his cubs?

To answer, you must look at his Scottish Presbyterian roots.

Porridge. Shortcake. Haggis. Boiled meat with potatoes.

A cub can be spatchcocked, spread out roasted with carrots, laid on a bed of nsima porridge. Lion cub meat may be shaved from the bone and sandwiched between shortcake. Boiled in a stew. Cooled into glue.

Haggis. Cub's brains are delicate, as are their liver and hearts. Fry in groundnut oil and place between layers of nsima, then roll into a lamb's stomach. Cool, then slice and serve with various crudites and salad vegetables.

My darling, says my husband. This is madness.

My darling, I say. I cannot stop myself

Later Livy comes to visit with her mother. We sit in my

study and have tea. Livy has a bruise on her face. She ran into the edge of the dining room table her mother says. Livy smiles at me. Are you writing the poem?

A poem for Samosa, I say.

We laugh.

Livy's bruise is a fat splotch of blue, green and yellow.

How are you writing it? Livy asks. Her little fingers tap my papers.

Don't touch, Hanora tells her.

You will read all of that to Kamuzu?

Yes, I answer. All of it.

My husband says, it is a disease in you, in all you poets. Why must you write these words? I tell you that if you drive out of Zomba and along the highway you will come to Mikuyu prison where all you poets are held. Cheek to wall, feet to bone, bone to ground.

Did you know he beats his family?

Who?

Our neighbour, Hugo.

Impossible, he is a good friend. He fixed my car. He is an English lecturer.

Impossible for Kamuzu to be dishonoured. He is our saviour. He has the soul and blood of the lion. He has a wife and many female attendants, because if his wife's womb fails, another must be used.

Impossible for my words to exist.

I drive out by the prison. There is no one to be seen. All of them are held in Kamuzu's prison chambers, his torture rooms, or dead and buried in a patch of ground beyond the kitchen house.

Rule 9. Prison is for Poets, Defilers and Murderers

A shout above our bodies.
Turn to your other side.
So we turn. Once a night.
Right then left, fitting into the stink and shoulder of our neighbour and someone cries.
We cry so much.
We turn like sardines and cry.
What are you? women asked me when I entered this cell. A poet? They laughed. Touched my bleeding face, my broken toes. Ai ai ai, you will heal as a cripple. I? I murdered my husband. It was a good murder. I drew a machete across his face, then I split his stomach in two. There was so much blood I could bathe my feet.
I? I defiled my neighbour. I watched her every day and I loved her. I loved her skin and her eyes. I loved her as she shopped in Kandodo. I loved her.
I? I wrote a poem. Hail The Great Samosa.
Eeeeeeh, oh my poet woman, you will die here.

Rule 10. Poets Must Not Talk

Hey Poet,
Hey Poet, Kamuzu is not happy.
Hey Poet, Kamuzu is your gentle father.
Hey Poet, do you want to die?
Hey Poet, is your tongue necessary?

LA HÉBUTERNE

S ardines.
Stilletto.

Snow.

Cold floor.

Rats.

My blue dress.

Dedo on the bed. Dedo dying.

His skin is so hot then it is cold. His lips are grey.

He is insisting that he might live. I hold his head.

No one has come. My bones are light and loose.

Get up. So I get up. Dress. So I dress.

I tighten Dedo's scarf about his neck. I don't want him to talk but he talks.

'Has anyone come?'

'Not yet.'

On the first day I went down to Ortiz's apartment again. I knocked and called his name. I thought, surprise me please Ortiz, or even Hanka. Open the door and stand there with your nose wrinkled. Yawn and say, *What is it, Jeanne?* I stood for long minutes thinking how I would answer. I would say, I am really quite alive, can't you see and Dedo is insisting that he also will remain alive.

We are eating sardines and the rats are drunk on marc.

We need food. We have used all the coal and it is freezing now.

'They are away,' a man said from another door.

I went back to Dedo. Ortiz would arrive soon, I lied to him then I went to the window and leaned outwards. The tree was black and naked. The air was wet. A dog was pissing in the street. Dedo began to sing but he made no sense.

Dedo likes to put his hand on my belly. It makes me into a Madonna, he says. It makes me like his mother whom I have never met but I have read her letters. She is the only one you love, I told him, and he laughed. Lunia said, *of course he only loves his mother. All men do. You just have to be a good enough copy, then you can survive as his wife.*

A rat skits by my toes then sticks its head into a sardine tin.

When Lunia was last here, she smoked a cigarette and said how much she admired me.

Dedo glanced over at me. *You see?* his eyes said.

Lunia is Polish, dark and rich with lips and skin. Dedo has painted her clothed, but I see how easy she might disrobe from her dress, and coo 'Modi', and her skin would brighten hard on his easel, yellow hard and her teeth would show through her red lips.

I begin to draw. I draw a line. Then another.

My first lover was Foujita. We kissed. He said I had no qualms about a man's naked skin. He admired how I drew the body. The dip from above the shin to the dip above the ankle, the angle of hips, the nudes in the Académie Colarossi bent and stretched, and I could draw their lines, I could almost feel the moist plush of their skin if young, or their dry and withered limbs if old. The stove smoked, cigarettes smoked, sweat filled the air and sometimes my breath did not want to come out because what would have to come in to take its place.

After Foujita, there was Modigliani. There was the Carnival of 1917.

There was Chana Orloff and she introduced us.

He lifted my hair, bowed and his red scarf smelled of wine.

'I will draw you.'

Chana warned me. 'He sleeps with you all.'

I have drawn a stiletto. It protrudes from my heart. I cross it out and begin again. I draw the studio. I begin with the place where I sometimes stand so Dedo can paint me. I try to draw the sounds into my lines as well as the light. I try not to draw like Modi. A friend once said she could not tell our work apart and I shrugged and said what of it? Yet part of me rose up into my throat. *I paint more than he does. I paint landscapes. I have painted Soutine as he could be if he was not as Dedo sees him. And Dedo can no longer sculpt. I have spooned Aphrodite's stomach and buttocks in clay.*

'I will draw you,' he said.

After that he slept with me.

After that I had to sew up my underclothes.

I was nineteen. He was thirty-four.

He took drugs and he drank.

He painted women while he drank.

I left my parents' house.

My brother André remonstrated in a letter to me posted from the Front.

My mother haunted the hotels Dedo and I slept in, and my father could not believe that I had thrown myself to a Jew.

Dedo refuses a cup of warm water.

'Wine.'

'You could go back to Italy, Dedo.'

'Like this? Like a nothing?'

I hand him a bottle of wine and he drinks until he has the strength to stand.

'I will go to the Rotonde. I will find Soutine.'

He moves forward then halts, sways and falls to his knees. We crawl back into our bed. I kiss the sores on his face and press his lips with my finger. He has only a few teeth and his gums are soft, dark pink and rotting.

He says, '*You* are everywhere I look.'

Get up. So I get up.

Pick up an empty sardine tin, and I do.

I put it on the window ledge.

There is wet, fat snow outside.

The dog is shivering.

Leave, Jeanne. Leave now.

The rats watch as I walk around the studio and Dedo mumbles in his sleep. I visit the lavatory and I feel my baby lie low near from where I pee. I close my eyes and imagine myself in the Rotonde, myself and not Dedo, myself and anyone else, myself drawing what I see, the smoke and the drink, the plates of eggs, the small dark coffee cups, the wine glasses, then the faces. So how to put a face where it belongs on my sketch paper, the lines and hollows, paunches and the plain bald skin of the body, tiny moustaches, battered teeth and broken eyes?

Dedo groans from the other room. I wipe myself, then stand and the room lists sideways. My joints hurt. My mouth fills with warm water from my belly.

When I had returned from Nice and told him of the new baby still as tiny as a fish in my womb, he stared at me from inside his long stare.

'We do not have luck.'

The night outside is black.

The rats are constant...

A Jew, my father said. *A Jew?*

Dedo laughed in his face, *Yes, I am a Jew. And your granddaughter is half a Jew. We are everywhere, Monsieur Hébuterne.*

The light from the landlord's window is dark yellow like the skin of Lunia Czechowska's neck in Dedo's paintings. My first baby cried so much. There were days when I tried to live with the crying but there was something in me, a dark rotting anger that spread from my heart and into my eyes.

The Zborowskis said I was ruining the great Modigliani and now I was pregnant again. What could Modigliani do with another mouth to feed?

And Lunia took my first baby to live with her in the Zborowskis's apartment.

She said it was to give me peace.

Peace was emptiness. I held my Aphrodite's stomach and buttocks in the palm of my hands, and I saw how Dedo's cigarette smoke had turned my sculpture grey. I mixed colours and I painted. I painted him. I painted the tree outside. I painted death as she lay in my bed. If I went outside, I saw people talking about me.

Imagine giving away her baby. And him — his opium and wine, do you not hear him tumbling up and down the stairs? Did I not hear that he grabbed her once by her long hair and sought to kill her in the Luxembourg Gardens?

I am drawing a stiletto.

I drink some marc wine, open a sardine can and spoon out some fish with my index finger. After a while I throw up into the lavatory, then I sit against the wall and I listen to Dedo sing about Italy and his mother. How she loves him, her darling Amedeo, how he will return with money from the London Exhibition, and me, his gentle wife with blue eyes, and our little Jeanne Modigliani, fat from a nurse's milk.

Lunia was sold for 1,000 francs in London.

The Zborowskis liked me again.

They were certain that Dedo would be rich.

My ankles twist a little as I walk up and down the studio. I cannot sleep. My bones are unsteady. I smell of sardines and wine. Dedo stinks of sweat and piss and the sores on his face glisten like rounds of yellow gold with dark and weeping ruby centres.

Leave Jeanne. Leave.

So I leave.

I walk down the staircase, out into the courtyard. The dog slinks to my heels, looks at my face then whimpers away. The cold air holds fast all the smells that I can smell. The gutters are thickened with a little frost. A woman walks by without any glance at me but she is holding a bag of potatoes and I am surprised that I am no longer hungry. I am full to my very edges with fish. My teeth hurt. My throat is sick.

I wander to the Rotonde. It has people inside so I enter the warm, sweaty air and guide my belly in front of me as I look for a seat. Kisling glances up at the air but not at me. Valadon rubs her eyes. Picasso and Cocteau are seated in a corner. I go up to them and say,

'Dedo is dying.'

They gaze at me.

'Dedo is dying,' I tell them.

They pour some wine and drink, talk of nothing so I turn away. A man approaches with flowers for his lover. A woman retrieves an olive from her breast. The long spread of table legs, the scrape of shoes, a shout, a kiss, a scream of either love or hate and the air fattens with sound and smells and I crave paper and a pencil to sit and sketch as Dedo once did.

He drew portraits for wine. He kissed my lips and I tasted that wine. He was clean and beautiful. We danced and he held my hair in his fists and ran his teeth upwards to my scalp. It was joy then. He loved my quietness, so I kept my quietness. His friends remarked my secretive eyes, so I kept myself behind my eyes. My father accused me of being next to a whore and my mother said, *you think this is love, all this running between hotels, all this life in cafés with the demi-monde, those people who drink from the gutters and reek of each others' bodies?*

Their priest reminded me of the Holy Spirit.

I replied that Dedo had the Holy Spirit in his blood.

When the war was over, my brother André disowned me.

When the war is over, Dedo promised, *I will bring you to my mother.*

He will destroy you first, Chana Orloff said. *All those models he sleeps with, all their paintings, don't you tire of seeing their faces much like the faces from those African sculptures that he covets. He longs to mix his fingers into stone. Modi wants to be Renoir.*

And there is Simone, the one before you, Jeanne.

Tubercular Simone loved Tubercular Modigliani.

She had blue eyes and blonde hair.

She was Canadian and lived in Paris.

She spent her money on Modigliani.

Tubercular Simone became *enceinte,*

Tubercular Modigliani *l'a laissée.*

You smile now, Chana said, *yet he will destroy you.*

Sardines.

Cold floor.

Rats.

I pick up my stiletto.

Sardines.

Stiletto.

Cold mouth.

Dedo sits up and taps his chest.

'My lungs,' he says.

His breath crackles and cries.

He calls for 'Mario'.

I sit behind him to prop his arm as he puts touches to his painting of Mario Varvogli. The rats nuzzle the empty sardine tins, and Dedo hums a little as he examines the black of Mario's hat and tie. He coughs hard and shoves the edge of our sheet into his mouth to prevent any blood on the painting. His ribs billow in and out, the shiny pustules of his face seep yellow and I clasp his shoulders to hold him straight.

The silence is cold and waits for me to speak.

'Remember how you painted Diego Rivera?' I say, 'with his fat face and his lazy, half-looking eyes?'

Dedo nods.

'It was him as he really was, not how you wanted to see him.'

I say that terrible truth then I say more.

'In Haut-de-Cagnes you painted landscapes. We ate olives and good fish, and you licked the oil from your fingers and placed them into the paint, and it was as if you lifted the sun into the canvas. It made my bones warm to see you disappear into those paintings, but then you found another woman.'

*An Italian too, Mother said, grubbing out on the side of a hill.
How many children has she, ten or twelve? And how she has
spread out, squat like a human pig, sinful despite all their Holy
Roman history and their signs of the cross. I see him. Scram-
bling his way to her so they can lie like pigs in muck and straw.
She will have a belly made by him soon enough.*

    And he isn't even a Picasso!

I painted the bright sun-bleached ground of the hillside and
Dedo, a speck of dark, his scarf dashed red from his neck
climbing to the Jacobelli's farmhouse. I painted the sea. I
searched for the correct blue, not like my eyes, but deeper yet
with sunlight reaching down into the cold and reflecting upwards. It is a dangerous blue. A blue to disappear into and not
return, and as I sat before my painting, I thought how easy it
would be to be free again, to discover something else to love
instead of a man or a god.

    Dedo screamed at me to disappear with him. He hated
this southern light, this sea and the smell of the earth. He
wanted Paris again.

Remember Paris, Jeanne?
    Remember the oily twilight,
    the lamps outside the Rotonde,
    soup in Rosalie's, the café light,
    wine and the long windows of
    our studio in rue Grand Chaumiere?
    Remember the tree you painted?
    How its branches twisted

like arthritic fingers...
Love me because you dare.

Remember the poverty, Jeanne.
He sleeps with his models, Jeanne.
Remember God.
Remember your father, your brother.
Remember you must hide your sin.
Remember being a girl.
Remember being you.
Remember the bed you slept in.
Innocent. Innocent. Innocent.
Until taken by a Jew.

The landlord's wife yells outside for her son and I go to the window. Although she does not see me, I put my hand outwards, and I notice that the rain goes through my skin and lies inside my flesh. I am drunk on marc, starving for vegetables. I am seeing the moon as it slips sideways. I want a tomato in my mouth, an aubergine with fresh mint and cheese. Dedo is dying.

'Don't leave me,' Dedo says.

He watches me from the bed. He wants me to hold him but he smells. My stomach heaves and I have to visit the lavatory. Nothing comes up, yet my stomach pushes against my throat. My breath stops. My heart fills my ears and I am being strangled from the inside. I pound my fists into my neck. My eyesight darkens.

DAMN YOU
DAMN YOU
DAMN YOU

DAMN YOU to him.

DAMN YOU to me.

Live without virtue, he had advised me and we spun dancing in the dark Paris streets. We made love in beds perfumed by pots of urine hidden in small cupboards. My father railed the priests against me. My mother told me I was soiled.

DAMN YOU

DAMN YOU

Everything is silent, even the rats, yet slowly there is the sound of the water in the lavatory and my vision clears while my body turns hot then cold. There is a window above the lavatory and it sits in its deep brick setting, light pink with swathes of yellow through the paint that continue beyond the sill and outwards onto the lavatory wall.

A small voice speaks from the window.

'You are just a little painter.'

'I am an artist,' I say.

The voice laughs. It sounds like Zborowski and I stare at the window, trying to make out his face but there is nothing there.

'I painted Soutine,' I say. 'Smelly Soutine, a man who knows no manners and I put him against a wall, a beautiful wall full of colour and I painted him as someone who knows who he is deep inside. Stealthy Soutine, Streetwise Soutine, *my brother*, Dedo called him.'

There, I told Dedo. *See, that is him. We painted him side by side, but see what I have found out?*

Soutine preferred Dedo's painting. It was he, right to the tips of his hair.

Yours is good, Jeanne, *but it is not true.*

Someone is knocking on the door, calling Dedo's name. I run to open it and there is nothing except an empty landing and staircase. I decide to visit the de Zárates but there is no answer. The walls follow me as I climb back up to the studio, and Dedo is conversing with the rats in Italian. I drink some wine and smoke a cigarette. Dedo is convinced that he has recovered, even though the blood that comes out from his mouth is thick and smells of iron.

He puts back his shoulders and his hair. 'I should be in Midi by now.'

'With Lunia,' I say.

'She is good for me, Jeanne.'

'Those are the Zborowksis's words in your mouth.'

'I need to get well, Jeanne.'

'She wants you, Dedo.'

'She is good for my art.'

'I am good for your art.'

'You are a mother. You are my fiancée. You are sacred. You are everywhere I look.'

He reaches for a brush. I pick up my stiletto and we play like this, he with his brush and me with my stiletto. He paints the air and I jab at my fingers until pricks of blood appear.

Remember your poetry, Jeanne?
    Remember how you read
    in bed?
    Sometimes nursery rhymes,
    sometimes not?
    Sometimes Apollinaire,
    Sometimes rot?

Remember Zborowski, Dedo?
He prefers the dying to sell.
Ortiz de Zárate told me so,
He waits for your death knell,
Your wonderful dealer Zbo.
I was timid, sweet and gentle,
You twisted my hair and loved
my eyes, my flair oriental,
I would save you, they all said.
And now we are almost dead.

Dedo coughs blood and laughs. He clasps our hands and promises that we will be bound in eternity. He sleeps and I undo our hands. I think of many things. I think of love and of finding Dedo, as if I had found God, and my heart had peeled open under his smile. Now the rats nudge the sardine tins on our bed. Open another, Jeanne. Feed us, Jeanne.

I sleep. I sleep and...

Ortiz de Zárate comes to us on the seventh day. He cries down to the landlord to bring soup but Dedo vomits blood and Ortiz has to call for the ambulance.

'I have only a little bit of brain left, Ortiz.'

Kisling sends a telegram.

'It is all up with Modigliani.'

And women watch over me in a hotel room paid by Zborokowski.

I am allowed to see him the next day and my father accompanies me. Dedo is laid out quiet and dead. I kiss his face then I walk backwards from his body and Kisling opens the door. Father takes me home and puts me in my old room. Mother gives me milk. André sits with me until he falls asleep. The night comes into our courtyard and I decide to disappear into its black colour. I walk backwards through the open window. I hold my belly and the air rushes cold under my arms. I walk back into the dark, like the Greeks walk, seeing the last of everything. I walk back until there is nothing and later a workman finds what is left of me, puts me into his cart and takes me to the front door. My brother André tells him to take the body to rue de la Grande Chaumiere. His mother must not see that sad and broken thing in the cart.

'Who is she?' the cart man asks the landlord after they lay me on my bed.

'La Hebúterne,' the landlord answers.

They leave me there.

Sardine tins.

Rats.

My blue dress.

Snow.

Cold night.

My blue dress.

Get up. So I get up.

Dress. So I dress.

It will be morning soon. We have sardines and marc.

And later I will buy aubergines and cheese.

Later. Yes later. Oh, life is good.

The rats are happy amongst the sardine tins. See how they skittle, Dedo?

My bones are light and loose.

There is something on the bed but I will not look at it. I have to work on a painting, a bright white canvas there on the easel but I cannot hold my brush, charcoal or crayon. I laugh because my fingers are nothing. My skin is nothing. I blow my breath and nothing comes and in the dark behind me the door opens and clicks its latch. Someone is coming in and I don't want them here. I touch my canvas and see all its tiny holes, then a rat runs over my eyeballs. It is such a strange sensation! I blink its little feet away from me but it insists on nipping my nose. Its eyes glance over mine. There is a shape in his eyes. A man in the doorway, tall with Dedo's hat, like Death as I painted him once.

Dedo, let me go. I have work to do.

I look at the bed where my body lies, where the rats nuzzle the last of my warmth under my arms. They nestle and nip at my breast. Modi, no arms... no kisses... not now... I have to work... and if I am buried there will be nothing left of me... I wish to go back.

Dedo, let me go...

I should have lived.

Oh... I should have lived.

THREE HOUSES IN ROME

There were three houses in Rome facing a green courtyard in the Quatiere Garbatella, *lotto 10* on Via Luigi Orlando. They had been built there, among many others, in the 1920s to house workers for the trains and the seaport. The tallest house was terracotta coloured. It had a squat black door with two large windows placed across its front face and at night two lamps lit beneath the windows cast shadows up against three gargoyles' heads put there years ago to protect against evil. This house joined onto the smallest of the three, washed pink with one window set atop a long black doorway. It looked like a happy house, and the windowsill was painted green. It had no gargoyles. The third house, just as tall as the first, was coloured a darker pink with two windows on either side of the doorway. The dark pink façade was freshened every spring in time for tourists or for television crews who often came to film the Italian life they wanted to see. An alley way existed between the third and second house where cats often congregated, screamed or miaowed.

The concierges of each house, Lorena, Amedeo and Pietro, met for wine and cigarettes in the evenings in the small communal courtyard across from their houses. They discussed their three sets of foreigners who lived in them.

The first house contained an Irish family who had arrived in Rome during the last year's lapses in Covid lockdown. For them the food in Italy was ideal. There were bakeries, grocery shops, bars, and restaurants. To Lorena, the daughter had clean blue eyes. The mother was a mystery. The father was a self-blinded fool. The son was an idiot and neophyte thug.

Amedeo controlled the second house. His tenants were a brother who was an artist and a sister who worked as a media journalist, and Amedeo laughed at their consternation at the house's sloppy plumbing. He told them to fill pots from the night before and if things were bad in the morning at least they could wash their armpits, face and genitals.

'In my opinion, he is not an artist,' Amedeo said. 'He permits his paints to drip on my staircase. Blue, red, green, and black. I gifted him with cleaning products, but nothing has happened.'

'His sister is handsome,' Pietro, the third house's concierge, said.

Lorena stretched and yawned. She was tired many nights now. She shivered in the winter breeze. Her husband was thirty-five years buried and she slept with a framed photograph of him on his Vespa in 1964 outside his house in Ostia. She smiled as she remembered him now. His hands, his long toes, his smell, his long tattoo of a fish from his left wrist to his left shoulder. The fish's mouth was open and received a woman's first finger. Her finger, he often told her and others.

'Goodnight,' she announced.

Amedeo and Pietro followed suit, each to a separate ground floor compartment in each of their houses. Pietro halted at his door, cocked his head, and listened to the silence, then he climbed the stairs to his tenants' door to listen more. Some nights he heard piano music but most of the time he was disappointed with their lack of drama. The husband had a disease, and the wife did not make herself friendly to anyone. Pietro did not trust them. They also complained about the plumbing, the terrible sun in the summer, the smell of fermenting piss in the alley between his and Amedeo's house. He told them not to worry.

'Men must relieve themselves. Like the cat and the dog.'

The husband's face, hands and neck were covered in dried white-fish scale-skin which, if not pasted with Vaseline, fell onto his glasses, his shirt collar, his sweater sleeves, and lay like thick white dust on the tips of his shoes.

Life in each house began early. The mad artist Sutton whistled as he bound down the stairs and out into the street. His whistle faded once he entered the local cafe for his morning coffee. His sister, Claire Sutton, took a quick shower, switched on the kettle, made toast, then dug into the Nutella jar. She breathed deep and felt the bony-ness of her hips before filling her mouth while scrolling her phone. A body had been discovered on one of the beaches in Ostia, her brother's favourite painting ground. The news video roamed from the flat dull sea to a rubbernecking crowd and back to focus on the dead body of a young man in a dark leather jacket with yellow seams on its sleeves. The voice-over reported that the young man was a drug addict but perhaps someone was missing him, someone who was praying for his safe return.

Lorena, seated on a stone bench a few metres from her door, now observed the daughter and son of her house rush out, she for university and he for the small gang of thugs he loved. They collided with Sutton who was returning from his coffee. The boy laughed and his sister grabbed his arm.

Sutton pushed into their faces. 'Hello Sorcha,' he smiled. 'And you get fucked, Cormac.'

'What did you say, you Aussie shit?'

'Cormac!' Sorcha warned.

Lorena shut her eyes and pretended sleep.

'Don't think I don't know what you've done. It's all over Ostia.'

'What is?' Sorcha asked.

'Your pseudo-gangster brother killed a man yesterday.'

'Oh yeah?' Cormac said. 'Who saw me?'

'I just heard the facts, mate.'

Now, Lorena thought then opened her eyes to see Cormac drive his fist into Sutton's face. Sutton crumpled, his right ankle twisting hard beneath him as he landed on his buttocks. Lorena, watching, laughed out loud. She adored fights. The crunch and the sweat.

Cormac kicked Sutton's face. 'Want to watch that mouth of yours, Sutton. Come on, Sorcha.'

Sutton scrambled to his feet and wiped blood from his mouth. He saw Lorena watching. He spat. 'Bloody crazy old bitch.' He side-stepped a woman who had just exited Lorena's house. 'Morning Mrs Farrell.'

Jude Farrell nodded at the bleeding man and thought well, he's alive so why should I bother asking?

'Ciao Lorena.'

'Ciao Signora Farrell.'

Lorena never had much to say to the woman, who sometimes returned with odd men on certain afternoons. She was a mystery.

Jude Farrell exited the local café with cigarettes and a bottle of sparkling water. She walked to the Metro, boarded the train into Rome and did what she did every day. She played at being a tourist for the first hour, the statues, the incense, the vast paintings where life naturally had that Frederic Fellini glow for most of the time until she chose an outdoor cafe to sit and wait for some man to discover her. Oh yes, she is slightly chilled by the cooling temperature — how observant — and yes, she adores Rome, the churches and the plazas and, after a while yes, he could buy her lunch, and simply yes, why not accompany her back to Garbatella to learn some English?

Cormac halted his scooter at the wrong university building and Sorcha put her hand on the scooter's ignition.

'Cormac.'

'He's lying, Sorcha.'

'Cormac.'

He twisted her wrist off the ignition key and enjoyed her pain.

'But what if I did kill that guy? What if it was the greatest feeling I ever felt?'

Every evening so far and in front of the three houses, Lorena, Amedeo and Pietro sprinkled salt and pepper over roasted almonds and cashew nuts. They dunked their cheeses into a bowl of pesto, then peeled plums for sweetness.

'Ciao,' Sorcha greeted them.

'Ciao signorina.'

She sat down amongst them. Pietro kissed his fingers towards her. *Bella mio eh?*

Sorcha paid attention to the insects in the green shrubs as Pietro asked her if she had found a lover yet

'No.'

Lorena slapped his ears. *Idiota!*

A voice called down to them from the second house. 'Ciao. Shall I bring vino?'

Claire Sutton floated from the house in a summer dress covered in a lace cardigan. Amedeo stood and raised his hat to her. He was seventy and had a full head of black hair. She held up her bottle of wine and he accepted it with a bow.

Pietro grunted because he was chewing nuts.

Sorcha took out a notebook and jotted something down. No one noticed.

Lorena flicked her crooked fingers over her misshapen crochet, counting the missed stitches, then unravelled her work back until she was satisfied.

Claire Sutton said, 'Lovely work, Signora.'

Pietro grunted. 'It just gives her fingers exercise.' He shrugged at Lorena's look. 'Her mind is separate of course.'

Sorcha had heard about Lorena's madness from the café owner. Ah, you'll stay at Lorena's house? That crazy old woman who still loves young men. Lorena believes she is descended from Lady Garbatella, you know? Sorcha knew. Everyone knew the large Art Deco graffiti and heard the story from Lorena.

'See the lace?' Claire asked Lorena now.

Lorena picked up her lacework from the table. It hung in clots, yellow from her cigarette-smoked, arthritic fingers, and still Lorena gripped her crochet hook, shoving it into each stitch, her tongue out over her lip, in out, in out as Sorcha watched, unaware she herself was being watched until she looked up and met Claire Sutton's smile.

'I notice you're jotting down words.'

'It's just something I do.'

Claire Sutton reached a hand under her long hair and elevated it. Amedeo smiled at the gesture. He liked the curls and sprigs that stood out from her temples. She was a long woman, barefooted tonight, gold necklace and earrings, white dress tightened by a brown leather belt.

'Are you trying to be a writer?'

'No.'

'Your notebook is so obvious. I saw it straight away.'

Claire Sutton then remarked upon the body found in Ostia, on the beach. Throttled to death, she told them. 'I'm doing a story on it,' she announced.

'Vino,' Pietro suggested. Amedeo stood and poured Claire Sutton's wine into each glass. They all drank, eyes on eyes and smiling into their wine.

Sorcha's notebook was rolled up in her left fist and the tip of its wire spine dug into the flesh between her thumb and index finger. The more it dug, the more her own spine straightened. She felt unreal but at least she had her spine.

'I love these evenings,' Claire Sutton said but before her sentence ended a long roaring sound began and came closer, the sound curved sideways, grew louder, roared in circles, screams and laughter, motorcycles, and car tyre squeals.

Amedeo cried *Degenara!*

They're doing wheelies, Sorcha said.

Lorena spat.

Amedeo and Pietro also spat, missing Claire Sutton's shoes by millimetres.

Ragazzi e ragazza...stupidi e pericolosi

Claire Sutton stood up and redraped her wrap. 'That's your brother. Buona notte all'

Sorcha remained seated on a stone bench, waited there until a scooter hummed its way into the lotto and steered through the obstacle courses of stone benches, walkways, and steps. A girl sat behind Cormac, her legs splayed over his.

Amedeo and Pietro shrugged at each other, arose and walked to their houses. The scooter curved round them, spitting dust and small stones. Amedeo made the sign of the devil, then disappeared. Pietro glanced up and noticed that one of his tenants, the husband, was watching from his window. Pietro waved but the man backed out of view.

'They are the last,' Pietro promised himself. 'No more strange ones.'

Lorena left her crochet in a pile on the stone, then walked into the scooter's path. She laughed as Cormac gunned his scooter in loops and circles. *Demone!*

Cormac wheeled his scooter around the old woman, round and around. His girl threw back her long hair. *Sì sì amore mio!*

Ground dust spurted up into Lorena's face. *Bastardo pazzo!*

Cormac circled Lorena once more then braked, grabbed her grey hard hair, and shoved his mouth on her face. 'Sono un dio,' he yelled against her teeth.

I think we're all mad here, Sorcha thought as she walked past her brother and Lorena standing there, a sated smile on the old woman's face, Cormac laughing. How does it happen, Sorcha thought. How does it all become a horror film? Just an extended holiday, her father had promised. It was still her father's excuse despite everything being wrong.

Our marriage is dead, her mother had declared.

Our son is insane, she told her husband.

Our daughter keeps everything in her head.

Her mother had said it in a screaming spiel, but Sorcha chopped it up, wrote it down in her notebook, recited the words to herself and told herself that one day she would be free of this family, free to be someone cut neatly away to live her own life.

That's not true, a little voice told her, but just don't think about it.

Signor and Signora Asquith lived in Pietro's house. Signora Asquith shopped at night in the Carrefour supermarket and neither she nor her husband ever really explored Garbatella. They had moved in a month before the Suttons and the Farrells and had insisted on fitting blackout blinds to the windows; then they paid for the whole of winter season.

According to Pietro, Mr Asquith suffered from a disease not unlike leprosy. 'The man's skin sloughs off like that of a snake. When she goes out at night, her husband sits at an open window. When they leave, I will have so much skin to sweep.'

According to Amedeo, Signora Farrell came upon Signora Asquith in the courtyard one night perhaps four to six weeks ago. It was one of the last very warm nights and Signora Farrell was cooling herself near the bougainvillea, drinking a large glass of something containing mint leaves and slices of lime. She hailed Signora Asquith who was returning from Carrefour. You could tell that Signora Asquith was uneasy, but she accepted Signora Farrell's invitation to sit with her. Amedeo was working on the hinges of his house's front door and could not hear any of the women's conversation, but he did happen to see Signora Farrell raise her hand and call out ciao to Signor Asquith who was sitting at his window.

According to Lorena, Signora Farrell has now taken to sending her daughter to Signora Asquith with a gift of Irish soda bread.

According to Sorcha, Mrs Asquith invited her to sit for a cup of tea and cut the bread into doorstep slices for her husband, scraped on butter and covered it with morello cherry jam.

'We live near Windemere,' Mrs Asquith said, and Sorcha branded the words into her mind to write them later. 'It's in Cumbria and it has the largest natural lake in England. My family ran a farm there for years, but I ran away from all of that and married Tom from Yorkshire. You must think I am so strange to marry a man with Ichthyosis Vulgaris. They call it the fish skin disease.'

According to Mrs Asquith, Mr Asquith was having a good day. His skin was not flaking too much. It was pink and tight beneath a thick transparent cream. His wife stroked lanolin across his eyelids and blew skin cells off his eyelashes

According to Sorcha, Mr Asquith was in thrall to Mrs Farrell's genius soda bread making.

'Poor old sod,' Mrs Farrell said. 'If he only knew I get it from Dunnes and it's two days old.'

According to Pietro, when the police arrested Cormac, the boy's father followed them to their car, begging for his son's freedom. 'He sounded a mad man. He screamed about the plague.'

Sorcha had followed Cormac and the police down to the bottom of the stairs. Her father was shouting about a plague. Her mother was screaming that it was all her husband's fault.

'An extended holiday in Rome you promised us and look what has happened now. Sorcha, tell your father he has ruined us!'

Her mother remained at the top of the staircase and continued to scream.

Sorcha wanted everything to be quiet so that she could tell herself that nothing was real; that everything was a mad and terrible dream. Yet she could see the smallest wrinkle on one of the policemen's faces, and then Cormac turned and embraced her goodbye.

According to Lorena, a young woman should not have to amuse a married man whose skin was falling from him and not while she was suffering from the truth about her murderous brother.

Amedeo and Pietro advised Lorena to say nothing.

In the beginning, Signor Farrell had been a quiet man full of nothing to say except greetings. An architect on a working sabbatical with one of the most brilliant firms whose premier client was the Vatican. A man who, not unlike the mad artist Signor Sutton. every morning entered the café bar and ordered an espresso. He drank it fast, called out ciao, bounded from the doorway and in minutes was in his car to drive across the Tiber.

'He was living his dream,' Amedeo said.

Lorena ran her lips across her teeth. That boy had ground his lips against her mouth. His breath. Oh, his breath, and now her skin tingled like a girl's. She would visit the boy in prison.

Pietro watched Lorena's face. 'You are an old woman,' he reminded her.

According to Lorena, she waylaid Signor Farrell one night when he returned from work. He stood a few steps above her on the staircase, tired and weaving from wine. He listened to her concerns then said,

'In three hundred years, they'll talk about the plague to begin all plagues.'

His eyes were glass-blue like his daughter's. Lorena caught the banister so as not to fall because of them. Her head was light, and the walls stirred around her. Something cold opened in her chest and she had to step back down to level ground.

'It's opened our heads and let some demons out.'

A mad man, Lorena realised. A mad man and his family are renting my house.

'Buona notte,' she said and walked away, keeping a sideways glance upon him until she was safe behind her apartment door.

He entered his apartment at the top of the stairs and found his wife asleep on the couch, his daughter was reading in her room. He poured more wine and sat in the kitchenette. The world was cracking apart and he could not stop laughing.

Mr Asquith wanted to know about Ostia Antica. What is it like to wander where ancient and ordinary Romans wandered? Imagine the miniscule stones that caught between their sandaled toes could catch between yours. What do you do, Sorcha? Where do you sit, Sorcha? What do you smell, Sorcha?

She liked his soft voice. It sounded like Yorkshire.

She told him that she walked along the Decumanus Maximus to the Porta Marina and stepped into taverns, shops, and houses. Details, he asked her and walked with her, first stopping at the theatre to imagine what it must have been like to sit and watch a play by Terence the Famous or someone of his ilk, then walk along the avenues and call into one or many of the thirty-nine wine bars to buy ready-to-eat meals with wine.

They laughed and plopped olives into their mouths.

Sorcha walked miles within Ostia Antica and brought back photographs and written sketches to Tom Asquith. She focussed on contrasts of colour, space, depth, and height. The sun-brazened, broken ochre walls of the Capitolium, the chalked pink and grey facade of the House of Fishmongers and a bakery, the House of Millstones. She described the deep orange- and terracotta-coloured frescos in a house in the Insula Delle Case a Giardino, black and white mosaic floors describing an octopus trapped in a dolphin's mouth, scorpion-shaped horses carrying Neptune, the wheel ruts on the Decumanus Maximus, various frigidariums including one with a mosaic of Venus rising from the sea to wring her hair dry while a many-footed lobster, as well as long-tailed serpent, looked on.

'Venus Anadyomene,' he said

Venus's body was straight and thick, her right leg crooked at the knee, strands of her red-brown hair caught in her left hand and tightened about her right bicep.

Tom Asquith smiled at Sorcha.

Sorcha did not smile at him.

Earlier Mrs Asquith had mentioned that Mr Asquith was always fully moisturised so he should not flake too much if he ever touches you, my dear.

His fingers were smooth, although swollen and shiny, and they roamed from her notebook over the table's glossy veneer and onto her hand. Sorcha did not move.

Mr Sutton waylaid Sorcha as she left the third house, the house with the fellow whose skin continually fell off and asked her if she cared to look at his work on the three houses. He arranged his sketches, watercolour, and gouache as well as charcoal, on one of the stone benches.

'They're good, 'she said.

'But choose, Sorcha. Choose.'

She looked at all of them.

'Charcoal.'

'What?'

'Charcoal'

He laughed. 'Bloody charcoal.'

The three houses stood in charcoal. Lorena's gargoyles leered too forward on the canvas. She liked how he accentuated their teeth and eyes. They seemed to be watching Lorena, Amedeo and Pietro there in the garden with their night vino. Sorcha positioned herself there but looking towards the alley between the second and third house. Coldness moved inside her. She pulled her stomach muscle to her backbone.

'My brother didn't kill anyone' she said.

He glanced at her. 'Okay.'

The café owner across the square waved over at them both. The sun remained warm, but the breeze was cool. Sorcha asked, 'Why would he kill anyone?'

Sutton gathered his art. 'How would I know?'

'Sono un dio,' Cormac had told her, breathing close to her ear just before the police took him away. He told her that he had sensed it just the moment before the boy died. He could have held his thumbs back, hauled the boy up and pushed him away but a hot red colour sluiced through his eyes and his ears, and he ran his thumbs up and down the boy's trachea then pressed it until Pop!

Claire Sutton smiled at her. 'I've found you.'

Sorcha was sitting in the communal garden near the bougainvillea and palm trees, vomiting up her third expresso, a thin, beige, grey coffee whey. Her vomit spread over snippets of twigs, ants and tiny stones.

'Jesus,' Claire Sutton sighed. 'And now I have such bad news about your brother.'

Pop! Sorcha remembered.

Sorcha laughed because she knew. Claire stood out of her way, mindful of the girl's stupid laughter and her vomit. Sorcha, still laughing, walked across the courtyard to the alleyway between the second and third house. She leaned into the dark there, pressed her elbows and wrists against the stone wall, then her face and laughed and laughed against the stupidity of everybody's world.

ACKNOWLEDGEMENTS

Acknowledgements are due to the following publications in which versions of these stories first appeared: *gorse; The Cormorant; The Lonely Crowd; The Purple House Anthology: The Music of What Happens* (New Island); *Galway Stories: 2020* (Doire Press); and *TSS Publishing*.

I wish to acknowledge the genius art of Charlotte Salomon's *Charlotte: A Diary in Pictures* (Collins, London 1963). Her life and death inspired my story 'Life or Theatre'.

I owe a real debt to my family who have had to live with a writer. They say they don't mind but I know they must have gritted their teeth sometimes. I love them and could not do without them.

I would like to especially acknowledge the kindness of other writers, namely Elaine Feeney, Alan Mc Monagle and Mike McCormack. It is wonderful to receive their encouragement and their words and be in their company.

My gratitude goes to Lisa Frank and John Walsh of Doire Press for publishing *Three Houses in Rome*. It has been a lovely experience and they have my utter respect and admiration.

I would like to acknowledge the Arts Council of Ireland for awarding me an Agility Award in 2021 towards the completion of *Three Houses in Rome*. This award not only aided me in my work, but it also granted me space and time thus enhancing my writing life.

ABOUT THE AUTHOR

ÓRFHLAITH FOYLE is a short story writer, poet and dramatist and lives in Galway. *Belios*, her debut novel, was published by Lilliput Press. Arlen House published her short fiction, *Somewhere in Minnesota* and *Clemency Brown Dreams of Gin*, as well as her debut poetry collection, *Red Riding Hood's Dilemma*. Her work has appeared in the *London Magazine*, *The Dublin Review*, *The Lonely Crowd*, *Wales Arts Review*, *The Manchester Review*, *The Stinging Fly*, *gorse* and various anthologies. She wrote and directed the radio dramas *May's End* and *How I Murdered Lucrezia*, which were both adapted from her short stories and received full BAI funding, as well as premiering on Newstalk Radio in October 2021 and 2023, respectively.

Órfhlaith received a full Arts Council Agility Award in 2021 to complete a first draft of *Three Houses in Rome* and was awarded a full Arts Council Literary Bursary in 2022.